BLACK HISTORY SPEAKS

The drums of Africa
still beat in my heart.
They will not let me rest
while there is a single
Negro boy or girl without
a chance to prove his
worth.

Mary McLeod Bethune
Quoted in the New York
Herald Tribune (May 9, 1955)

ARD WINNER

Mississippi CHALLENGE

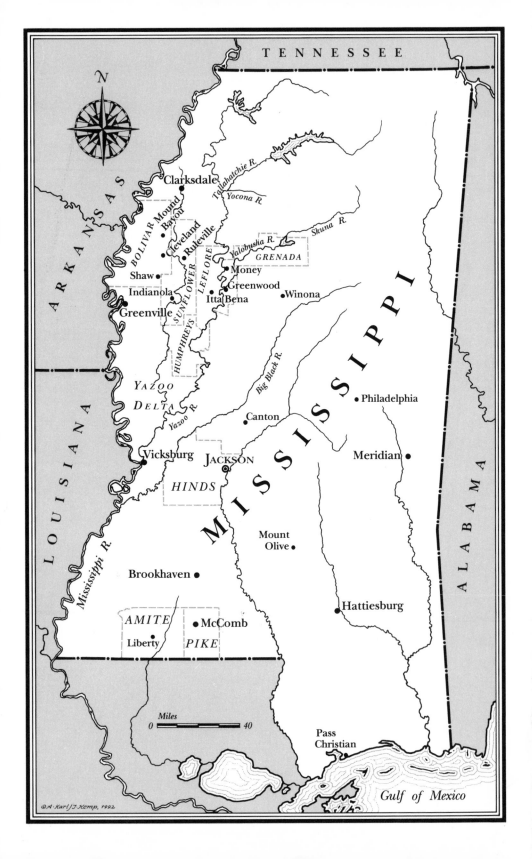

TENNESSEE

N

ARKANSAS

Clarksdale

Tallahatchie R.

Yocona R.

BOLIVAR *Mound
Bayou*

*Cleveland
Ruleville*

Skuna R.

Yalobusha R.

GRENADA

LEFLORE

Money

Shaw

SUNFLOWER

Greenwood

Indianola

Itta Bena

Winona

HUMPHREYS

Greenville

YAZOO
DELTA

Yazoo R.

Big Black R.

Philadelphia

Canton

MISSISSIPPI

Vicksburg

JACKSON

Meridian

HINDS

LOUISIANA

Mississippi R.

Mount
Olive

Brookhaven

ALABAMA

AMITE

McComb

Hattiesburg

Liberty

PIKE

Miles

0   40

Pass
Christian

©A·Karl/J·Kemp, 1992

Gulf of Mexico

Mississippi
CHALLENGE

by Mildred Pitts Walter

Bradbury Press   New York

Maxwell Macmillan Canada   Toronto
Maxwell Macmillan International
New York   Oxford   Singapore   Sydney

Bradbury Press
Macmillan Publishing Company
866 Third Avenue
New York, NY 10022

Maxwell Macmillan Canada, Inc.
1200 Eglinton Avenue East
Suite 200
Don Mills, Ontario M3C 3N1

Macmillan Publishing Company is part of the Maxwell Communication Group
of Companies.

First edition
Printed and bound in the United States of America
10 9 8 7 6 5 4 3 2 1
The text of this book is set in Baskerville. Map by Jim Kemp and Anita Karl

LIBRARY OF CONGRESS CATALOGING-IN-PUBLICATION DATA
Walter, Mildred Pitts.
Mississippi challenge / by Mildred Pitts Walter. — 1st ed.
p.   cm.
Includes bibliographical references.
Summary: Describes the struggle for civil rights for the blacks in
Mississippi, from the time of slavery to the signing of the Voting
Rights Act in 1965.
ISBN 0-02-792301-0
1. Afro-Americans—Civil rights—Mississippi—Juvenile literature.
2. Civil rights movements—Mississippi—History—Juvenile
literature. 3. Mississippi—Race relations—Juvenile literature.
[1. Afro-Americans—Civil rights—Mississippi. 2. Civil rights
movements—Mississippi—History. 3. Race relations.] I. Title.
E185.93.M6W24   1992
305.896'0730762—dc20   92-6718

For Jesse Morris, the unsung hero.
He did the job in a quiet, astute way,
without seeking glory.

CONTENTS

This photo was taken in the late 1870s.

UPI/Bettman

Mississippi
CHALLENGE

Fannie Lou Hamer became one of the leaders of the Mississippi Freedom Democratic Party. Here she addresses the
1968 Democratic National Convention.

UPI/Bettman

PREFACE

In 1960 in the South, African Americans decided that they were, in the words of Fannie Lou Hamer, "sick and tired of being sick and tired" of the lack of equal opportunities and denial of access to the ballot. They had long wanted to participate in the political process to determine their destinies and the destinies of their children. In the sixties they decided to take direct action and legal steps to gain their voting rights.

This book is about that direct action in the state of Mississippi and about how, for almost a century, black people in that state struggled just for the right to vote.

That struggle went on in a closed society either un-known to or ignored by the outside world. Then in 1961 the Student Nonviolent Coordinating Committee (SNCC) entered the state. In 1963 the Mississippi Freedom Democratic Party (MFDP) was organized. Those two organizations, working together, changed the course of Mississippi history.

It is not an easy task to bring alive the events that made the Mississippi Freedom Democratic Party a unique historical organization. There is little documentation. It is painful, because the struggle that led to President Lyndon Baines Johnson's signing of the Twenty-fourth Amendment (the Voting Rights Act), guaranteeing the right to vote without penalties, and without payment of poll taxes for primary and other federal elections, was a war that left many casualties on only one side. To fully understand what happened in Mississippi from 1960 to 1965, one must know the history of that state and of the people in the struggle. This book reveals that history from the time of slavery to the time of the Emancipation Proclamation and Reconstruction, that period immediately after the Civil War when the South was restored to the Union. We move through two world wars up to the day when SNCC decided to begin a voter registration drive in Mississippi in 1961. Reviewing this history is also painful, for it is not (as some historians have led us to believe) a story of a peaceful, orderly, industrious clime where blacks sang happily as they broke their backs and tore their fingers picking millions of bales of cotton. Mississippi was not a place where white southern ladies and gentlemen spent leisure time entertaining and being entertained, sipping mint juleps, and dancing reels in their mansions. No. From its early existence, Mississippi was a place where fear, tension, hatred, and hard work were the rule; a place where poor whites struggled against a huge slave labor force that in its discontent created an atmosphere in which the masters felt safe only with an armed militia.

Most history has two points of view: one that is told as it is seen through the eyes of the ruler, and another told as it is seen through the eyes of the ruled. The story of MFDP is told through the eyes of the ruled. It is a story that needs telling. And it needs telling from the perspective of those who struggled.

One may protest that there are protective laws, specifically the Thirteenth, Fourteenth, and Fifteenth amendments. The Thirteenth Amendment freed the slaves, the Fourteenth made African Americans citizens with certain rights, and the Fifteenth granted them the right to vote. And there is the Bill of Rights, which protects the rights of all Americans. These laws were all in existence when the Voting Rights Act was written as the Twenty-fourth Amendment to the Constitution, to do what the Fifteenth Amendment should have done.

What we must clearly understand is that laws that are not enforced do not achieve the purposes for which they were intended. Laws have meaning only when they are unmistakably part of the institutions and experiences of a people. The story of MFDP shows that the Fourteenth and Fifteenth amendments were not a part of the institutions and experiences of the people of the United States.

I have a reason for revealing the struggle and the challenge of the Mississippi Freedom Democratic Party. It is to give you, the reader, an opportunity to see the disastrous consequences of closing one's eyes to oppression and refusing to actively insist that laws guaranteeing freedom, justice, and peace are upheld.

Here detailed are *planned* social and economic conditions that white Mississippians forced upon black Mississippians. Perhaps you may think that too much emphasis has been placed on the hangings, beatings, tortures, and murders, but, to quote two SNCC workers, Lawrence Guyot and Michael Thelwell, "It is only from this perspective—not one of individual and irrational acts of racism, but one of rational, organized, and programmatic oppression on the part of the power machinery of the State, that the plight of Mississippi's black population, and the MFDP response to it, can be understood."

Writing this book has not been easy. It was accomplished only with the help of many people. To those who made the task less difficult and more possible, I owe acknowledgment and thanks for support and encouragement.

First of all I owe a debt of gratitude to all in the movement, especially those young people in SNCC who risked their lives in Mississippi to encourage people to register to vote and to transport them to polling places. Much appreciation is due to those brave African-American citizens who faced economic punishment and reprisals—loss of their homes, their jobs, and their land. Thanks to Margaret Carey, Director, and the staff of the

Voting Rights Project of the Center for Constitutional Rights, in Greenville, Mississippi. They gave me valuable information on MFDP.

Appreciation is due to the Society of Children's Book Writers critique group in Denver, who helped with their suggestions; to Mary Folsom, who read the manuscript with a keen critical eye; and to my son, Earl, and my grandson, Nizam, who also read the manuscript and encouraged me when the task seemed most difficult.

My appreciation, too, to the staff of the Denver Public Library for their unrelenting searches, and to my editor, Barbara Lalicki.

Thanks to Lawrence Guyot, Robert Parris (Bob) Moses, and Diane Nash Bevel for their courageous struggle and, after all these years, for still being willing to let their lights shine. I am grateful for their remembrances and suggestions.

Part One

If you miss me at the Mississippi River
And you can't find me nowhere
Jus' come on down to the swimmin' pool,
I'll be swimmin' there.

—*Freedom song*

1. *SIT-INS, STAND-INS, WADE-INS, AND KNEEL-INS*

On the first day of February 1960, four African-American freshmen at North Carolina Agricultural and Technical (A & T) State University at Greensboro, said yes and no simultaneously. Junior Blair, Frank McCain, Joe McNeil, and David Richmond sat down at a lunch counter to say yes to self-determination, freedom, and justice; and no to segregated public accommodations, separate and unequal education, separate churches, and unjust treatment under the law. Word of their daring confrontation spread, and within days, other students in South Carolina, Virginia, Florida, and Tennessee were staging sit-ins, too.

1

Students in Nashville were inspired and led by James Lawson, a thirty-one-year-old graduate student at the school of theology at predominately white Vanderbilt University. Lawson had visited India and was aware of the long nonviolent struggle (1919 to 1948) Gandhi had waged to gain India's independence. Of course, nonviolent direct action had been used in the United States as early as 1943 by the Fellowship of Reconciliation and by the Congress of Racial Equality (CORE) to end discrimination in public places in Chicago, Baltimore, and St. Louis.[1]

The Nashville students, with help from CORE and the Southern Christian Leadership Conference (SCLC), held special training sessions in nonviolent tactics. Instead of hitting back, the students were taught to control their anger and do these things:

1. Make every effort to protect your head;
2. Protect others by placing your body between them and the abuse;
3. Do not strike back or curse if abused;
4. Do not block entrances to doorways or aisles;
5. Act courteously and friendly at all times, but do not hold conversations with floor workers;
6. Remember love and nonviolence.

On February 13, 1960, over five hundred students gathered at Fisk University to be transported to the First Baptist Church in Nashville. There they received last-minute instructions in nonviolent tactics and were dispatched in small groups to lunch counters in the downtown area.

John Lewis, a student at American Baptist Theological Seminary, told of his experience:

> We went into the five and tens—Woolworth, Kress, McCellan's. . . . We took our seats in a very orderly, peaceful fashion. The students were dressed like they were going to a big social affair. They had their books, and we stayed there at the lunch counter preparing our homework, because we were denied service.[2]

Another student, Diane Nash, a native of Chicago attending Fisk University, participated in that first sit-in in Nashville. She gave this account:

> In our [nonviolence] workshops we had decided to be respectful of the opposition, and try to keep issues geared toward desegregation, not get sidetracked. The first sit-in we had was really funny, because the waitresses were nervous. They must have dropped two thousand dollars' worth of dishes that day. We were sitting trying not to laugh because we thought laughing would be insulting and we didn't want to create that kind of atmosphere. At the same time we were scared to death.[3]

WHY NONVIOLENCE?

Many of these high-school and college students who sat in were young—fifteen to twenty-two. Most of them were black and poor. Many, like twenty-one-year-old John Lewis, were sons and daughters of farmers; some were the sons and daughters of sharecroppers (sharing the crops they tended and harvested with absentee white landowners). Some came from families where the mothers worked in the homes of well-to-do white people. Some of their fathers were factory workers and truck drivers. With rare exceptions, they attended all-black schools. Most of them were Christians, their movement planned and dispersed from churches in their communities. Being southern and closer to their African roots, they believed that they were one with the universe and that the group, *we,* is far more important than the individual, *I.*

Nonviolence, which many believed in for religious reasons, was also, in a violent society, a practical tactic.

James Lawson:

> Why non-violence? The most practical reason is that we are trying to create a more just society. You cannot do that if you exaggerate the animosities. Martin Luther King used to say, "If you use the law, 'an eye for an eye and a tooth for a tooth,' then you end up with everybody blind and toothless."[4]

Because they were so young, they were not taken seriously at first. Yet, because they were black, many whites, unaccustomed to having blacks say no, were frightened. The whites responded with harsh, brutal treatment. John Lewis described one incident:

> We got a call from a white minister who had been a supporter of the movement. He said that . . . the police would stand to the side and let a group of white hoodlums and thugs come in and beat us up, and then we would be arrested. We made a decision to go. We all went to . . . Woolworth's in the heart of the downtown area, and we occupied every seat at the lunch counter, every seat in the restaurant, and it did happen. A group of young white men came in and they started pulling and beating primarily the young women. They put lighted

Participants at lunch-counter sit-ins were threatened, hit, and often had food poured on them by angry customers. Whites who participated were often treated more harshly and stared at in disbelief.

UPI/Bettman

cigarettes down their backs, in their hair, and they really started beating people. In a short time the police officials came in and placed us under arrest, and not a single member of the white group, the people that were opposing our sit-in, was arrested.

That was the first time I was arrested. . . . To go to jail was to bring shame and disgrace on the family. But for me it was like being involved in a holy crusade, it became a badge of honor. . . .[5]

Again, Diane Nash:

The movement had a way of reaching inside you and bringing out things that even you didn't know were there. Such as courage. When it was time to go to jail, I was much too busy to be afraid.[6]

Diane went to jail again and again. Seeing how much money was being spent on bail to get students released, she came up with the idea of "jail, no bail."[7]

Even without a well-formed organization, hundreds of students sat in, waded in at public pools and beaches, knelt in at segregated churches, and stood in at segregated movie houses. More than thirty-six hundred were arrested. The most remarkable thing is that while they were being burned, beaten, and jailed, they sang. New words to old songs they had sung all of their lives became their battle hymns:

Ain't gon let Sheriff Pritchard turn me round

Their spirit of love and their songs baffled the enemy and wore their jailers' patience thin. Young men on the chain gangs and young women in the jail cells schooled themselves in ways to carry on the struggle when they were let out of jail.

6

SNCC IS BORN

As the activities attracted more and more participants, older leaders in the African-American community sensed that the students were serious. The students confronted those who practiced racial discrimination in a nonthreatening way. This type of confrontation is known as direct nonviolent action. The students started and maintained the struggle, and even without a tightly structured organization, their actions became a movement.

Ella Baker, a black woman who was born and educated in the South, recognized the vast historical significance of what was happening, and she moved to help the students organize. At the time, she worked as executive secretary in SCLC's office. A well-known civil rights activist, she had worked throughout the South in 1940, organizing National Association for the Advancement of Colored People (NAACP) chapters. With funds from SCLC and with the support of Dr. Martin Luther King, Jr., and Len Holt, an attorney from CORE, she coordinated a conference at Shaw University in Raleigh, North Carolina, April 15 to 17, 1960. One hundred twenty students came together and formed the Student Nonviolent Coordinating Committee (SNCC) on a temporary basis. In October of that year, at a conference in Atlanta, the organization became permanent, with Marion Barry as its chairman.[8]

Julian Bond, who was a student at Morehouse College, was impressed with Ella Baker's forthrightness at that conference:

I remember her speech, "More Than a Hamburger."

And I can remember it being an eye-opener to me because I really had not thought about much more than a hamburger. We were doing lunch counter sit-ins, we wanted to integrate lunch counters, and that was the deal. I knew that racial problems extended far beyond lunch counters. But I didn't see *us* doing anything like that until she mentioned it there. So it was a real eye-opener, a real step, a big leap for me.[9]

Those who wrote the first paragraph for the organization's statement of purpose did so within the framework of their religious upbringing:

We affirm the philosophical or religious ideal of nonviolence as the foundation of our purpose, the supposition of our faith, and the manner of our actions. Nonviolence as it grows from Judaic-Christian traditions, seeks [a] social order of justice permeated by love. . . .[10]

SNCC attracted thousands of young black and white students from the North and South. Such black leaders as Marion Barry, Sam Block, Julian Bond, McArthur Cotton, James Forman, Tom Gathier, Lawrence Guyot, James Lawson, John Lewis, Bob Moses, Diane Nash, Willie Peacock, Ruby Doris Smith, and many more, especially unnamed women, had their beginnings in SNCC. Their courage, strength, and tenacity are personified by Lana Taylor, a student from Spelman College. Lana sat in at a lunch counter in Atlanta:

The manager walked up behind her, said something obscene, and grabbed her by the shoulders. "Get the hell out of here, nigger." Lana was not going. She put her hands under the counter and held. He was rough and strong. She just held . . . her hands . . . brown, strained . . . every muscle holding. . . . All of a sudden he let go and left. . . . He knew he could not move that girl—ever.[11]

We shall not, we shall not be moved
Just like a tree planted by the water.

Though the reaction to the movement in North Carolina, South Carolina, Georgia, and Tennessee was brutal, there were positive results. Many lunch counters and other public facilities opened to African Americans. However, SNCC's most dangerous and unrewarding work was to come in Mississippi, where it helped organize the Mississippi Freedom Democratic Party (MFDP), which made the Mississippi Challenge.

I been 'buked
And I been scorned
—*Spiritual*

2. *MISSISSIPPI: A LAND OF CONTRASTS*

*B*efore one can begin to understand the jailings, bombings, economic punishments and denials, and deaths that African Americans suffered with the coming of SNCC workers into Mississippi in 1961, one must know some of Mississippi's history.

Many African Americans living in Mississippi had long felt that life was simply a struggle for survival. Most African Americans living outside Mississippi who had to visit the state, for any reason, were well aware that they visited under serious risk to their lives.

Just six years before SNCC workers started the voter registration drive in Mississippi, in 1955, Emmett Till, a fourteen-year-old black boy from Chicago, was

Emmett Till

murdered in Money, a small town in the Yazoo Delta. His body was found tied to an iron cotton-gin wheel at the bottom of the Tallahatchie River. In spite of overwhelming evidence, an all-white jury acquitted J. W. Milam and Roy Bryant, who had been accused of the murder. Later the murderers were paid four thousand dollars to tell how they had killed Emmett. The reporter William B. Huie published the story in *Look* magazine. No action was taken against Milam and Bryant. This was just one more added to the list of thousands of killings of blacks in that state, many never officially reported.

The image of Mississippi as a place where people are consumed with racial hatred may belie the reality of the state. It is not a monolith. It is a patchwork quilt, a land of contrast, where gentleness and violence stand side by side.

It is a land of hot, glare-filled days. During summer, steamy heat presses in from below, above, and all around. Amzie Moore, whom we will meet later, has said, "The weather is so hot you can almost see it. If the wind doesn't blow every once in a while and just bring you a little cool air, you look like you might be getting ready to burn to death. . . ." Even without the sun of dazzling days, the darkest of nights can be just as hot. Yet, between January and March, the moist air can chill to as low as minus two degrees.

The land once belonged to the Choctaw and the Chickasaw Native Americans. Tributaries from the river Big Black—the Skuna, Yalobusha, and Yocona—and the rivers Tallahatchie and Yazoo still have the names given to them by the Native Americans. The black, slow-moving, snake-infested rivers and the deep dark nights and hot brilliant days add to the mysterious environment of Mississippi.

The state has salt marshes and stretches of sandy beaches along the coast of the Gulf of Mexico. One cannot imagine the beauty of the lush green earth and sweet smells in the air during spring. The soil supports pine trees and groves of silvered, moss-covered oaks that hide old mansions and sprawling ranches. But just yards away from those magnificent showplaces are weather-beaten clapboard houses bleached white by sun and rain; there are cabins with torn roofs and tar-paper shacks with outdoor toilets and no running water.

That land lying between the Mississippi River on the west and the Yazoo River on the east is known as the Yazoo Delta. The floodwaters of these two rivers deposited sand, silt, and clay and formed an alluvial plain once said to be the richest known anywhere. The planters who came with their slaves early in the nineteenth century may not have known that deltas have been important to humankind since prehistoric times. The abundance of animal and plant life and the rivalry between rivers and the sea create the most dynamic situation in nature for the building of civilizations.[1]

What the planters must have known, however, was that the sandy loam mixed with clay was far more productive than the worn-out soil of the piedmont region they had left behind. With black slaves and poor white overseers, they built an empire on cotton, and the state of Mississippi, before the Civil War, became the richest in the nation.

Nobody knows the trouble I've seen
Nobody knows my sorrow
—*Spiritual*

3. COTTON AND SLAVERY

After the War of 1812, the peace encouraged movement westward. Settlers moved into the rich, virgin lands of the Gulf region and established cotton farms. Textile factories needed raw materials, and the demand for cotton boomed. Cotton became highly profitable, and by 1834, Mississippi, Louisiana, and Alabama were leaders in its production.

The population of slaves in the southern states grew rapidly. By 1860 it was about four million. Most of these slaves were owned by relatively few planters. In 1860 there were 384,884 slave owners, 338,000, or 88%, of whom held fewer than twenty slaves apiece. Of these, 200,000 owners had five slaves or less.[1]

Since thirty to sixty slaves made a plantation most profitable, few plantations in the South had a profitable working force. Of the plantations in the South with more than twenty slaves, Mississippi had the most.[2] With the use of the cotton gin and a large supply of slaves, planters in Mississippi made huge profits on cotton. In collaboration with factory owners in Birmingham, England, and factory owners in the eastern and northern states of the United States, planters made slavery an entrenched institution in the South, and in Mississippi, cotton became king. Dr. W. E. B. Du Bois, noted African-American sociologist, described the Mississippi plantation:

> The graciousness and ease of the plantation system had scarcely taken root there. Mississippi plantations were designed to raise a profitable cotton crop and not to entertain visitors. Here and there the more pretentious slave manor flourished, but, on the whole, the level of the state in civilization and culture was distinctly below that of Virginia and South Carolina.[3]

Where the number of slaves on a farm was less than twenty, the planters themselves managed their crops. They worked in the fields along with the slaves. On these farms, there was less brutality and loss of limbs and lives of slaves. However, when the slaves numbered more than twenty, white overseers were hired to manage the work on the plantations. These men were landless and often hated the slaves. They worked slaves from "can't to can't" (can't see in the morning until can't see at night).

15

Mansions like this one flourished on plantations in the
Deep South during the early nineteenth century. Blacks
referred to such a mansion as "the Big House."

New York Public Library

Overseers regularly searched slave quarters for weapons and for any kind of stolen goods. They enforced curfews, and anyone who left the plantation without a pass (a written note) from the owner was arrested. Runaways were severely punished. The treatment of slaves in Mississippi was so cruelly harsh that owners in other states found that the most menacing threat to recalcitrant slaves was a promise to sell them "down the river" to the Yazoo Delta.

From 1820 until the Civil War, cotton remained king. Only nature could hamper it. With not enough rain, the cotton bolls would not open, and if there was too much moisture, the bolls rotted. Getting rid of indigenous grasses, weeds, and insects utilized a lot of slave labor.

Although free African Americans in the North protested, there was no movement to end existing slavery or the importation of new slaves.

SLAVES FIGHT BACK

Gabriel Prosser, a Virginia slave, planned to attack the white establishment in Richmond in 1800. Gabriel made plans for months and swore to secrecy his black followers (about forty thousand slaves) living in the region. On the very evening it was to start, a great storm with torrential floods and gales doomed their rebellion. Richmond was placed under martial law, and many slaves were imprisoned. Gabriel Prosser was publicly hanged.

In 1822, Denmark Vesey, who had bought his own freedom, is said to have planned the most extensive slave uprising ever recorded. He was betrayed by a slave who worked in the house of the master. Vesey, along with thirty-six others, was killed.

The only well-known revolt that came close to succeeding was led by Nat Turner in 1831. Deeply religious, Turner believed he had been chosen by God to lead the slaves out of bondage. Some sixty whites were killed in Southampton County, Virginia. Word spread of the revolt, and whites, terrified, killed more than one hundred blacks, some involved in the revolt, some not.

Fear of the slaves provoked terror, and strict laws were created to prevent more uprisings. Slaves were forbidden to move about even for short distances. Everywhere plantations used hired patrols that exercised brutal authority. With uprisings and rumors of revolts, more and more stringent laws were passed to protect whites and to discipline blacks.

These laws were known as black codes. They varied from state to state, but all of the laws were designed to show that slaves were property and should therefore be treated as such.

Slaves could not own land or any other property. They could not strike a white person, even in self-defense. They could not leave plantations without special permission. An enslaved person caught out of bounds could be brought back forcefully by any white person. In Mississippi, slaves could not "blow horns or beat drums."[4] The drum was a means of communication for a people who were denied contact with any person who spoke a common language. Without verbal communication, and without the drum, many felt hopeless.

THE MISSISSIPPI BEAT

Along with the use of overseers to enforce slave discipline, planters used patrols. In Mississippi, counties were divided into areas called beats, where white males were required to serve for one to possibly six months. Their charge was to apprehend slaves found away from the plantations and either return them or put them in jail. Even today in Mississippi, the smallest political area is known as a beat. In spite of all the laws and restrictions, some slaves still rebelled, using arson, poison, and other means to vent their frustrations and seek revenge on unkind slave masters. However, as Meier and Rendwick point out in *The Making of Black America*, because of the harsh treatment, only 1.5 percent of all revolts between 1830 and 1860 took place in the state of Mississippi.

During this period of harsh treatment and uprisings, there were free blacks and whites outside the regions of slavery who saw the system as brutal and inhuman. They organized themselves as abolitionists and fought against the institution and helped many slaves to escape. As the situation became more tense, abolitionists became more insistent that slavery must be outlawed, or the nation would suffer dire consequences.

Then, on a Sunday night—October 16, 1859—John Brown led a raid on the federal arsenal at Harpers Ferry, West Virginia. He planned to take the town, distribute arms to the slaves, and lead a revolt throughout the South. With him were some twenty-one men, five of whom were black: Dangerfield Newby, Lewis Sheridan, John Cope, Osborn Perry, and Shields Green.

The plan failed, but it brought widespread attention to the atrocities of slavery and made eminently clear that the question of slavery had to be settled. There are those who believe that John Brown's raid sparked the Civil War.

The country became divided, and all other social issues—temperance, women's rights, and territorial expansion—paled in the light of slavery. The southern states were unified in their will to maintain slavery as an institution. By the time Abraham Lincoln was inaugurated as the sixteenth president of the United States, Mississippi and six other states (Alabama, Florida, Georgia, Louisiana, Texas, and South Carolina) had seceded from the Union. They formed a confederation and raised their own flag.

PRESIDENT LINCOLN HESITATES

The slave states bordering the Deep South remained in the Union, and the president moved with reluctant caution in order to hold them and to placate businessmen and other citizens in the North who believed slavery to be good for the country. However, Lincoln's Republican party had won the election on a platform that rejected further expansion of the slave system. Abolitionists pushed the president to act to keep southern planters from becoming even more powerful in federal affairs. Yet, as Lincoln admitted that slavery was the main cause of the Civil War, he still conceived as his most pressing duty the conservation of the Union, with or without slaves.

BLACKS BEG TO FIGHT

During the indecisive months between war and peace, free blacks implored the government to allow them to enlist in the Union army. They were rejected.

On April 16, 1861, Confederate soldiers fired upon Fort Sumter, South Carolina. Lincoln responded by declaring war. Four of the border states, Delaware, Maryland, Kentucky, and Missouri, seceded from the Union. Now eleven states were part of the Confederacy, but free black men who wanted to fight were still rejected by the Union army.[5]

The war created appallingly chaotic conditions for those held in bondage. All slaves did not become fugitives. Those who stayed on plantations were not allowed to become soldiers or military personnel in the Confederate army. However, they were used by the Confederates to grow, transport, and prepare food; to do military tasks; and to act as servants in military camps. Union generals knew that freeing the slaves would greatly weaken the Confederate army, but public opinion, North and South, was greatly opposed to arming slaves as soldiers.

In 1861 an act came into effect that said that any property used to assist in "aiding and abetting insurrection against the United States was the lawful subject of prize and capture wheresoever found. When the property consisted of slaves they were to be forever freed."[6]

This act caused the Union army many problems.

The army became responsible for food and shelter for slaves freed by this act, for fugitives, and for the care of those slaves wounded when caught in the crossfire. There was much confusion about what to do with these people who were considered property. From Mississippi alone there were about eight thousand:

> The fugitives had swarmed in from long distances, some of them carrying small children, none of them equipped for a long journey. All were hungry and weary, yet they seemed to be cheerful. . . .[7]

A Wisconsin soldier who watched them suspected that the average colored refugee had deep within him some sober thoughts, for all this surface gaiety:

> He was not only breaking up old associations, but was rushing out into a wholly new and untried world. . . . He was not certain of a full meal . . . even once a day, and he must have sadly wondered what would become of him. . . .[8]

Generals in the Union army granted some slaves an option: Stay on the plantations that had been deserted, or leave. Blacks not having that option, or just deciding to leave, streamed across Union lines. The government had no plans to care for these people, and nothing was done to prevent the inevitable chaos.

It was not until slaves became fugitives by the thousands, fleeing to Union camps, that blacks were finally permitted to join the Union army as soldiers. Some Union soldiers refused to cooperate in the "service of blacks." Some generals in the Union army were sympathetic. Generals Grant and Butler both devised plans whereby slaves were placed on confiscated Southern land and paid by the army to grow food for Union soldiers. However, by and large, those who followed Union forces suffered from hunger and exposure.

In 1862, Rufus Saxon, the commander of Southern Affairs, devised a plan to give blacks two acres of land for each working hand, with tools to cultivate it. That plan fell through. There was no land. "The government sold confiscated land to private parties. Eastern capitalists and philanthropists bought up a lot of southern land. . . ."[9] Controversy between the War and State departments over what to do with slaves created even more confusion. No one agency was responsible for the supervision and care of thousands of homeless and landless people. Consequently, many of them died. One Union official declared, "The mortality in Negro camps was frightful . . . most competent judges place it at not less than twenty-five percent. . . ."[10]

The refusal of the government to act on behalf of blacks during this period set the stage for much of the backlash that occurred against them in both the North and South during and after the war. White workers feared that any form of emancipation would bring a flood of blacks to compete for their jobs. Factory workers rioted in New York; in New Jersey white workers refused to allow black workers on the job; and in many cities black workers were beaten, harassed, and denied opportunities to work.

The war and the debate over freeing the slaves raged on. Abolitionists pressured for emancipation, but

President Lincoln still hesitated, declaring he could not free slaves under the Constitution. Lincoln also knew that he had little support to abolish slavery. Therefore, other steps were taken to solve the problem. However, an offer to compensate slave owners for their slaves did not work.

A few blacks were colonized in West Africa in a country called Liberia. But the plan of widespread colonization was to prove unworkable.[11]

In the meantime, the Confederates were winning the war. With the source of cotton for its textile mills greatly affected, Great Britain was ready to assist the Confederates if they gained ground in their push to invade the North. President Lincoln knew that Great Britain's support would assure a Confederate victory. He also knew that the working-class people of Britain were on the side of freeing the slaves. Du Bois states that "factories closed and more than half the looms and spindles lay idle. . . . Notwithstanding this, the English workers stood up for the abolition of slavery and protested against the intervention of the English."[12]

Pressure continued, and the president became annoyed when abolitionists accused him of being soft on the question of slavery. He wrote to his friend Albert G. Hodge,

> I am naturally antislavery. If slavery is not wrong, nothing is wrong. . . . And yet I have never understood that the Presidency conferred upon me unrestricted right to act officially on this judgement and feeling. . . .

In spite of the antislavery sentiment expressed in that letter, he later said:

My paramount object in this struggle *is* to save the Union, and is *not* either to save or to destroy slavery. If I could save the union without freeing *any* slave I would do it, and if I could save it by freeing *all* the slaves I would do it; and if I could save it by freeing some and leaving others alone I would also do that. What I do about slavery, and the colored race, I do because I believe it helps to save the Union. . . .[13]

The Confederates continued to win battles, and Union generals began to press the president to free the slaves. The generals wanted to deprive the South of the slave labor that was helping the Confederates win. The President drafted the Emancipation Proclamation, which his cabinet debated for two days.

Rumors of the possibility of a proclamation spread, and a cry rose up from proslavery Northerners. Some soldiers resigned from the field of battle, refusing to fight to free slaves. Then the Union achieved a victory or, as some historians claim, a military draw, at Antietam, Maryland. With this battle declared a Union victory, President Lincoln was politically able to call upon the Confederates to return to the Union before January 1, or risk losing their slaves. On September 17, 1862, he issued the Emancipation Proclamation, which stated,

January 1, 1863, all persons held as slaves within any state, or designated part of the state, the people whereof shall be in rebellion against the United States, shall then, thence forward, and forever be free.[14]

John Hope Franklin declared, "Working men in many parts of the world viewed this as a great humanitarian document."[15] "In England," Du Bois said, "as soon as Lincoln issued the Emancipation Proclamation, the workingmen . . . held hundreds of meetings all over the country and in all industrial sections and hailed his action." In light of this enthusiastic reaction, Britain's prime minister, Henry Palmerston, refused to recognize the South and declare war on the United States.[16]

That proclamation left the lives of four million slaves (five hundred thousand of them in Mississippi) in jeopardy, and those slaves who resided in states and select counties and parishes that were not in rebellion remained in bondage. Those states in rebellion were actually granted an option: Cease rebelling, rejoin the Union, and keep the institution of slavery intact. They had fully from September of 1862 to January 1, 1863, to act upon the option. They refused to return to the Union. On January 1, 1863, President Lincoln declared the slaves free.

Why didn't the Confederate states take Lincoln's option? Did they carry on the war to save their honor? Or were they trying to achieve a victory over the Union and make all of the United States slaveholding?

The underlying reason for their refusal may lie in the decision to fight on, which generals of the Confederacy made in 1864, when it was obvious that an end to the war was inevitable.

> An overturn was coming, and it was precisely the sort of overturn that the men who had created the Confederacy could not at any price accept. No peace based on reunion (the only sort of peace that was really conceivable) could be contemplated, because reunion, by now, inevitably meant the end of slavery.[17]

26

Southern generals felt great bitterness over the loss of so many lives on the battlefields and the loss of their property, including slaves. Therefore, when General Pat Cleburne suggested strengthening the Confederate army by recruiting blacks to fight on their side (guaranteeing freedom to anyone who served), one of the other generals responded,

> I will not attempt to describe my feelings on being confronted by a project so startling in its character—may I say so revolting to Southern sentiment, Southern pride and Southern honor.[18]

That idea was found unworthy of debate. One historian has suggested that

> . . . what Cleburne had quite unintentionally done was to force his fellow oficers to gaze upon the race problem which lay beneath the institution of slavery, and that problem seemed literally insoluble. It did not . . . seem possible to most men that white and black folk could dwell together in one community in simple amity. There had to be a barrier between them—some tangible thing that would compel everyone to act on the assumption that one race was superior and the other inferior. Slavery was the only barrier imaginable.[19]

The war between brothers, uncles, nephews, and cousins north and south finally ended on April 9, 1865, when General Lee surrendered to General Grant at Appomattox, Virginia. As in all wars, there were no victors among the poor. The political and pragmatic decisions that brought the end of slavery, the sometimes cruel and sometimes benign neglect of the millions of rootless, landless, and homeless blacks, tilled the ground for the new kind of terror that blacks faced in Mississippi from 1865 until 1960. Many good, honest, sincere, and intelligent citizens tried to avoid the great human errors and the tragedies that came about when, after the war, former slaveholders reclaimed power and created a new kind of bondage for African-American citizens.

A great human sob shrieked with the wind,
And tossed its tears upon the sea,—
Free, free, free.

—*W. E. B. Du Bois*

4. *ROAD TO FREEDOM*

Four million black men, women, and children sang a song of freedom, but they all had different skills, different abilities, different problems. Very few could read and write, and fewer still had any education beyond that. Many were field hands who had been cowed into submission; some with the physical scars of slavery were openly bitter and defiant. There were those who had served in the house. Some were the sons and daughters of their masters; a number had been educated abroad, yet remained in bondage. There were the few skilled seamstresses, tailors, and artisans who had been hired out to

29

make money for their masters. And there were those who had learned to survive by crafty means: lying, stealing, and deceiving.

Many of the former slaves must have feared the future. They knew no place other than the master's. As Pauline (Pearl) Howell, a slave, recalled:

> When freedom came, my mama said Old Master called all of em to his house, and he said, "You all free, we ain't got nothing to do with you no more. Go on away. We don't whup you no more, go on your way."[1]

It was the master who had given them information. It was he who had stood between them and the powerful forces of the law. Therefore, some who were offered the opportunity signed contracts as hired laborers and stayed on at the plantations. But many wanted land of their own. They wanted the fruits of freedom, the opportunity to know, to learn to read and write, and to make their own way. And so, most of them left their masters and became a people on the road, with few friends, no money, no land, few skills beyond farming, and very little education.

These newly freed men and women, with their children, roamed from place to place; or they became squatters in shelled, gutted buildings in cities. Some lived on deserted farms and plantations where unharvested crops had already rotted and livestock had perished from lack of care and food. Some were prey to returning rebel soldiers who blamed them for the war. All were in need of an organized plan to protect them, to provide them with land, and to direct them to the means of becoming participating citizens in a democratic republic.

Before the war, there were 488,070 free blacks in the United States. Of that number, 32,629 were attending school. Out of the total number of free blacks, only 91,736 were unable to read and write. Even in slave states, there were 3,651 black children in schools supported by free blacks.[2]

However, because of stringent slave laws that jeopardized the safety of slaves who were able to read and write and the safety of anyone who taught slaves, few of the four million newly freed blacks had acquired those skills. Less than 150,000 could read and write.

White abolitionists, such as Thaddeus Stevens, a congressman from Pennsylvania,[3] and Charles Sumner, a senator from Massachusetts, continued their demand for the just treatment of blacks. Stevens and Sumner, along with Frederick Douglass and other free blacks, knew that if emancipated slaves were to emerge as first-class citizens, they must have land, education, and the right to vote. They recognized the need for organized protection, immediate land dispersal, fair job contracts, and the issuance of food and medicine.

Finally, in March 1865, over the veto of President Andrew Johnson, a southerner who had become president of the United States after the assassination of Lincoln, and the objections of many, Congress set up the Freedmen's Bureau. The agency was placed within the War Department for a duration of one year after the war, but no funds were appropriated for it. The personnel were mainly soldiers, who knew nothing about social reform. The civilian staff members were all volunteers. Some of the bureau's responsibilities were to put laborers to work at regular wages; transport teachers, laborers, and officials; protect the rights of blacks to bear arms and to open schools; furnish land; and insure the vote for freedmen. Of course, southerners bitterly opposed the presence of agency personnel and made life difficult for them.

A year later, when a bill for the extension of the bureau was submitted to Congress, there was still much controversy. President Johnson was bitterly opposed to the bureau:

> Undoubtedly the freedmen should be protected . . . but by civil authorities. His condition is not so bad. His labor is in demand, and he can change his dwelling place if one community or state does not please him. . . .[4]

He vetoed the bill.

Black people realized that they were being forced to negotiate directly with their former masters and slave drivers for jobs and for civil and political rights. The president argued that in the South, where most freed slaves were located, peace had been attained.

Blacks protested. The veto was overridden. Some funds were appropriated and the bureau's time was extended to 1870.

THE BUREAU AND LAND DISTRIBUTION

In 1869 there were more than forty-six million acres of public land in the South. Mississippi had the least number of acres, approximately five million.[5] Petitions were signed asking the government to allot this land to former slaves. One such petition from the National Labor Convention, dated December 6, 1869, suggested that land tracts of forty acres each be allotted to freedmen.[6] As early as 1865, Thaddeus Stevens had recommended that land owned by seventy thousand southerners be confiscated by the government. "To each adult freedman should be given forty acres. . . ."[7] These petitions may have become the basis for the widespread belief of blacks that they would be granted forty acres of land and a mule. Many believed it was a promise. Any serious discussions about reparations for blacks' servitude still include the phrase "forty acres and a mule."

There was a lot of confiscated public land, but that land had been taken to prohibit expansion of the war, not to create a new social order in the South. Therefore, very few freedmen were given any of it. Some were permitted to raise crops on tracts of land on which they paid taxes. This included two-acre parcels of land that had been allotted in 1862 when General Sherman dispersed those slaves who were following Union lines. That land had been distributed without title—that is, no legal document entitled the person to it. Therefore, when the Confederates returned, the freedmen, who had been working the land for several years, were displaced. They ended up with no land at all. The process of restoration of land to southern planters was stepped up.

The Freedmen's Bureau controlled about 768,590 acres of land in December of 1865. By 1868, with the restoration, it controlled only 139,644 acres, and most of that was poor for farming.[8] Many former slaves had refused to sign contracts for work with former masters because they believed that they were going to get some acreage to work for themselves. This did not happen. They were called lazy and shiftless because they did not rush to farm others' property. They held out, believing that after having worked all of their lives making others rich, they surely each were worthy of a small parcel of land.

In spite of the failure of the government and the bureau, some blacks were able to acquire land through their own efforts. The most fortunate were able to take advantage of cheap land. These property holders were small in number, for it was difficult to raise enough money to buy even cheap land. Blacks who hired themselves out made as little as $89 per year, up to $150 during 1867 and 1868.[9] Often they were not paid in cash. Nevertheless, they were frugal, and many saved part of their earnings.

THE BUREAU AND EDUCATION

Although at first the Freedmen's Bureau Act made no provision for the education of freedmen, the bureau did give money from the rent of abandoned buildings to help in the founding of schools.

In 1866 another act, expanding the power of the bureau, benefited the existing schools that had been founded by the army, by religious organizations, and by freedmen themselves. A sum of $521,000, plus other sums that came from the sale and lease of properties that belonged to the former Confederate government, was allotted for educational purposes. In fact, the taxes and rents on land owned or leased by blacks raised $400,000 for the U.S. Treasury. This amount of money was used to support the bureau in its first year of existence.[10] During 1866 and 1867, black labor produced farm products, including two million bales of cotton, that brought more than $40 million in taxes into the treasury—much more than the bureau spent during its existence.[11]

With the support of churches—Baptist, Congregationalist, Methodist, Presbyterian, and Quaker—many teachers were transported from the North. A system of education was begun and spread throughout the whole South, benefiting both blacks and poor whites.

The black church played an important role in the education as well as in the health and welfare of the freedmen. As early as 1794, Richard Allen had founded the African Methodist church, and at the time of emancipation, many congregations were well organized in both the North and South, ready to help their freed brothers and sisters.

The Freedmen's Bureau and the missions from various religious groups organized and supervised schools from kindergartens to colleges. There were day, night, Sunday, and industrial schools that were always crowded. Often people had to be turned away for want of room. The churches and other societies spent $1,572,287. Over that same period (1868 to 1870), the bureau spent more than $3,000,000 on education.[12]

From 1865 to 1866, the teachers in all-black elementary schools were exclusively northern whites. Most were religious missionaries, sincere and hardworking. Gradually, black teachers were used to teach in all-black schools. During the first year of public education in Mississippi, there were more than 66,000 students and some 3,500 teachers, of whom 399 were black. Many of the students were Mississippi whites and poor white refugees from the war. They, too, benefited from bureau institutions.[13] Of the 1,700,000 black children of school age in the South, only about one-tenth were actually enrolled in school. Black children could only avail themselves of school when their parents were financially able to buy them clothes and to do without them in the fields. Yet, many southerners and northerners were astonished to know that from 1866 to 1870, freedmen contributed $785,700 in cash to their schools.[14] When the bureau closed its offices in 1870, 21 percent of the freedmen were literate.

THE FREEDMEN'S BANK

The Freedmen's Bank was created to serve blacks only. Two-thirds of all the deposits had to be invested in United States securities. The growth was extraordinary as deposits came in from day laborers, farmers, washerwomen, house servants, and mechanics. Before long, speculators in Washington became aware of the bank's growing assets. In 1870, they finagled Congress into amending the bank's charter. This change allowed one-half of the bank's funds to be invested in other notes and bonds secured by real estate mortgages. Money was loaned recklessly, and the former slaves, who had literally saved their pennies, lost it all.

At the date of closing, so far as is known, there were due to depositors $2,993,790.68 (almost three million dollars) in 61,144 accounts; this was never paid. The assets amounted to $32,089.35. The rest was represented by personal loans and loans on real estate which were practically uncollectible.[15]

Imagine the grief of those who had saved from meager wages earned washing and ironing, sewing clothes, and doing odd jobs. Farmers had kept their children from school to work on rented land, expecting that when they owned their own land, schooling would come. They had sacrificed everything, saving for the future, only to discover that their hard-earned money had gone into the pockets of the rich or been wasted on wild schemes.

We have come over a road
That with tears has been watered

In 1869, the work of the Freedmen's Bureau had already begun to wind down, and by 1872, it no longer existed. Many critics bitterly decried the money spent on freedmen. General Howard, the director of the bureau, estimated that "the total expenses of our government for white refugees and freedmen to August 31, 1869 have been $13,579,816.82."[16] During this period, blacks had paid more than double this amount in taxes. Yet some of the criticism was justified.

Investigations disclosed that certain funds had been badly handled. Fraud was committed by some of the bureau's thousands of agents, who were spread over wide areas without close supervision. However, the criticism of the bureau was so prevalent that Congress demanded a court of inquiry in 1874, which lasted forty days. The court reported:

> The world can point to nothing like it in all the history of emancipation. No thirteen millions of dollars were ever more wisely spent; yet, from the beginning this scheme has encountered the bitterest opposition and the most unrelenting hate.[17]

Commenting on the report, W. E. B. Du Bois said:

> This is perhaps an overstatement. The Freedmen's Bureau did an extraordinary piece of work but it was but a small and imperfect part of what it might have done if it had been made a permanent institution, given ample funds . . . and . . . gradually manned by trained civilian administrators. . . .[18]

With the bureau abolished and a president who had cast his lot with the southerners, against his own political party, Americans of African descent found a rougher road ahead.

> **I been rebuked and dragged about**
> **And put through the shackles so bad**
> **I done forgot some of my children's names.**
> *—Former slave woman Laura Clark*

5. *COTTON AND RACISM*

*M*ississippi *came out of the war with a severely damaged* economy. In 1860 the property in the state, not counting the slaves, was valued at $291,472,912. In 1870 it was only $176,278,890. The cotton crop came to 1,200,000 bales in 1860. It was less than half that in 1870.[1] Rather than address these problems, the legislators spent a great deal of their time fighting against plans that would bring racial and economic equality to the approximately 450,000 freedmen in the state.

As early as 1865, just when the war was over, Mississippi's ruling class had resolutely decided that African

Americans would not have citizenship status in their state. The appointed provisional governor at that time was William L. Sharkey, who took office in June of 1865. That same year, Mississippi hosted the first constitutional convention to be held in the South. One hundred representatives attended.[2]

The most pressing matter at that convention was not the state's economic decline or the plight of the state's 30,000 or more destitute blacks and poor whites—those whose very survival was in question. The chief concern was whether a black man should be allowed to testify against a white man in the courts. Setting a pattern that would still prevail a hundred years later, propositions presented to voters were determined by this one issue. When the election was over, the winners were those who were against letting black men testify in the courts. Benjamin Humphreys, a Confederate general, was elected governor, but he could not assume office because he had not been pardoned by President Johnson for participating in the secession of the state.

An ordinance was passed acknowledging the fact that slavery had been abolished in the United States, and therefore it did not exist in Mississippi, but the legislators would not be accountable "for what ever honor there may be in abolishing it."[3] They steadfastly refused to ratify the Thirteenth Amendment to the Constitution, which freed the slaves. The *Vicksburg Herald*:

> Shall Mississippi ratify the Thirteenth Amendment? We answer no, no, ten thousand times, no.[4]

The concession that slavery no longer existed in the

state of Mississippi was the only one made to African Americans. In October 1865, Mississippi's leading blacks met and protested to the U.S. Congress that the tactics of the planters, who were again in charge, were designed to reenslave them.

Republicans in the U.S. Congress were beginning to fear the arrogance of the Mississippi planters who had refused to ratify the Thirteenth Amendment. Led by Senator Sumner and Congressman Stevens, they pressured President Johnson to curb the planters' rising power. The president acted by suggesting to Governor Sharkey that those African Americans who were educated and holding property be given the vote.[5] That suggestion was spurned. The old idea that only white men were capable of ruling and that black men should not be allowed to vote prevailed. Ironically, much of the power Mississippi had in Congress came from blacks, because for the first time they were counted as citizens, thus increasing the number of congressional districts, giving more representatives to the state.

With tensions high between African Americans who were anxious to participate in government and planters who were determined that slavery was not over, whites began to fear the armed black federal troops in the state. In January of 1866, there were 8,784 black soldiers and 338 black officers. Planters complained bitterly, and Governor Sharkey claimed that the troops encouraged the belief among blacks that land was going to be distributed to them. President Johnson promised to move them as soon as possible. By May 20, 1866, all black troops had left Mississippi.[6]

THE RETURN OF THE BLACK CODES

With no armed blacks in the state, the legislature felt free to institute practices just short of reenslavement. The black codes, the penal and criminal laws that had formerly applied to slaves, were reinstated:

> Mississippi provided "That all freedmen, free Negroes and mulattoes in this state over the age of eighteen years, found in January, 1866, or thereafter, with no lawful employment or business, or found unlawfully assembling themselves together, either in the day or night time, and all white persons so assembling with . . . or associating with freedmen, Negroes or mulattoes on terms of equality or living in adultery, fornication with a freed woman, free Negro or mulatto, shall be deemed vagrants, and on conviction thereof shall be fined. . . ."[7]

Worse than that was the actual returning to their former owners of young people under the age of eighteen:

> . . . all freedmen, free Negroes and mulattoes, under the age of eighteen, within their . . . counties, beats or districts, who are orphans or whose parents have not the means, or who refuse to provide for and support said minors . . . it shall be the duty of the . . . court to order the clerk . . . to apprentice said minors to some competent and suitable person . . . *provided*, that the former owner of said minor shall have the preference when in the opinion of the court, he or she shall be a suitable person for that purpose.[8]

This was the beginning of the march back to slavery for many blacks in Mississippi.

Those planters who paid fair wages to blacks faced a backlash from poor whites who bitterly hated African

Americans and were loath to see them gain economic equality. Those decent planters were also in competition with others who unscrupulously paid blacks very low wages or no wages at all. At the same time, they felt great hostility toward those blacks who were being advised by the Freedmen's Bureau and supplied with northern capital.

Many southern states that had refused to ratify the Thirteenth Amendment also refused to ratify the Fourteenth Amendment, which guaranteed the civil rights of African Americans. Ratification of these two amendments was required for the states' reinstatement into the Union. Senator Sumner believed that southern states should not be permitted to rejoin the Union until they had presented state constitutions that declared the rights of blacks to vote and participate as citizens.[9]

Instead, many of the southern states reinstated the black codes. This action was an affront to those in Congress who had fought for fair treatment for African Americans. Many people felt that the return of slavery to the land where the blood of Union soldiers had flowed, and under which so many of them lay, would be a sacrilege.

In February 1867, Thaddeus Stevens presented the Reconstruction measure that divided the South into five military divisions. Mississippi was placed in the fourth district, with Arkansas. A provision in that Reconstruction Act granted blacks the right to vote. Each state was required to form a constitution that allowed for universal male suffrage, without regard to race or color. President Andrew Johnson vetoed the act just two days before Congress was due to adjourn on March 4. Nevertheless, with Stevens's leadership, the Reconstruction Act became law on March 2, 1867.[10]

Mississippi planters immediately began plans to prevent blacks from voting. General Alcorn (designated by the president to serve as governor) suggested yielding to suffrage and then controlling the votes of blacks, especially those who were isolated in rural areas. However, Mississippians still refused to ratify the Thirteenth and Fourteenth amendments.

In March of 1867, General Ord was sent to Mississippi to assume command. He abolished the black codes and made provisions for blacks and whites to register to vote. At that time 46,636 whites registered, and 60,137 blacks.[11] The first election was held that same year to choose delegates to frame a new state constitution.

The clear majority of blacks hardened the planters more against suffrage. Prior to the state Democratic convention, the majority of Democrats asked that their party refuse to participate in the proceedings. They took the position that no respectable white man could afford to take part in an election that allowed blacks to vote. A minority of counties refused to go along with this action and planned to take part in the election.

The first political-organization meeting that Mississippi blacks attended was the Republican state convention held to select delegates to frame the constitution. This so-called Black and Tan Convention was held in Jackson, Mississippi, in 1868. One hundred delegates were there, and although thirty-two counties had black majorities, only seventeen of the delegates were black.

bitterness was created by the clause that denied former Confederates the right to vote, and the Republicans declared that fraud and intimidation had been used by the Democrats.[18]

One of the first acts of Congress after the presidential election of 1868 was the authorization of the president to resubmit Mississippi's rejected constitution to a popular vote. The Democrats had no objection to the document if the disenfranchising clause was omitted. Blacks stated their willingness to work with honorable men and to give their support even to former Confederates.[19] In November 1869 the 1868 constitution was modified to provide amnesty for former Confederates, universal male suffrage, and encouragement of immigration. Other items remained intact, and the constitution was adopted. With a constitution and an agreement to ratify the Fifteenth Amendment, guaranteeing the right of blacks to vote, Mississippi qualified to be readmitted to the Union.

In January of 1870, the first Mississippi legislature under the Reconstruction Act met in Jackson. In spite of the fact that blacks made up 54 percent of the population, only 34 of the 140 members of the legislature were black: 4 in the state senate and 30 in the state house of representatives.[20]

John R. Lynch (not to be confused with James Lynch) was elected as Speaker of the House in Mississippi in 1872, but only after a deadlock had been successfully broken by U.S. senators Alcorn (formerly the appointed governor) and Ames. Five regular Republicans and two independents, who had been elected as state legislators on the basis of their promises to cooperate with the Republicans, refused to vote for Lynch because he was black. Senators Ames and Alcorn came from Washington and told the regulars that they were in honor bound to either support the caucus nominees or vacate their seats.[21] The independents, who were afraid that white voters would be offended if they voted for a black, were shown the irrationality of their thinking: They had been elected from areas where blacks were a large majority of voters.[22] Later that year Lynch was elected to the U.S. Congress.

In the congressional elections of 1880, James A. Chalmers challenged Lynch in the Sixth Congressional District. With marked ballots and fraud, Chalmers was declared the winner and given the certificate of election. Lynch decided to make a thorough investigation of the fraud and to contest Chalmers's seating. He carried the case to the U.S. House of Representatives.

In Issaquena County, Lynch had received a majority in every voting precinct, the returns being properly counted, certified, and returned by election officers. This information was then filed in the office of the circuit court. To insure Chalmers's victory, the county returning board illegally declared invalid all the returns except from one precinct.[23] Lynch collected certified copies of all the returns made by precinct officers, including certificates and tallies. With these documents, he filed a brief and made oral arguments before the House Committee on Elections in the spring of 1882. He won the appeal and was seated.[24] After that challenge, the Mississippi Democrats reorganized the congressional districts to insure Lynch's defeat in 1874.[25]

Along with Lynch, whose terms in the U.S. Congress spanned from 1873 to 1877 and from 1881 to 1883, two other African-American men served in that body: Hiram R. Revels, senator, 1870 to 1871, and Blanch K. Bruce, senator, 1875 to 1881.[26] Blacks were forceful in the Mississippi Republican party.

However, with the compromise of 1877, which made Rutherford B. Hayes president, white southern planters were restored to power. Blacks were disenfranchised and lost political clout.

From the very beginning of federal supervision to establish order in Mississippi, the Democrats, the party of former slave owners, had complained bitterly. However, with the Republicans determined that they were going to establish a just and democratic system with blacks and whites working together, some progress had been made.

There was much that needed to be done with little money. A whole new governmental administration, from top to bottom, had to be established. New schools had to be built. This was a formidable task, for most small towns and rural counties had no schools at all. Penal and mental-health facilities had to be built. With a tax increase, most of those things were done.

Contrary to statements that ignorant, power-hungry, inefficient blacks dominated the Mississippi government during the period of Reconstruction, the facts, as stated by Congressman Lynch, were:

> No colored man in that State ever occupied a judicial position above that of Justice of the Peace and very few aspired to that position. Of seven State offices only one, that of Secretary of State, was filled by a colored man,

until 1873, when colored men were elected to three of the seven offices, Lieutenant Governor, Secretary of State, and State Superintendent of Education. Of the two United States Senators and the seven members of the lower house of congress not more than one colored man occupied a seat in each house at the same time. . . . In the State Legislature there were never more than about seven colored men in the Senate and forty in the lower house. . . .[27]

In five other southern states, low numbers of blacks participating in Reconstruction government were also recorded.[28] Yet the propaganda persisted. Those few years brought great fear that, just maybe, African Americans were capable of learning and of exercising responsible citizenship. Fear and animosity and political greed increased Ku Klux Klan activity and gave rise to the White Knights, who intimidated, tarred and feathered, and lynched black people who sought to buy property, to maintain the land they owned, and, especially, to vote.

SHARECROPPING

More and more blacks were disenfranchised. Sharecropping became a way of life for most. On land owned by white planters, many blacks raised cotton with seed, fertilizer, and tools supplied by the landowner, who collected half of the crop and "expenses." Often expenses included rents for the shacks people lived in, food from the plantation stores, and other necessities. Often the black farmer had nothing at the end of the season except the need to go further into debt to the landowner. Consequently, the labor of the black farmer and his family

White-supremacy groups such as the Ku Klux Klan terror-
ized southern blacks without fear of arrest or prosecution.
New York Public Library

belonged to the landowner. Mississippi became a state of sharecroppers: doctors, lawyers, and teachers all depended upon the support of people, often the majority in a county, who earned no wages and paid no taxes.

By 1880 the South's cotton industry was restored. Whereas only 3,011,996 bales had been produced in 1870, there were 5,755,359 bales in 1880.[29] Terrorism increased along with this boom in cotton. With the rise of the Ku Klux Klan, whites deprived blacks of their rights without any fear of consequences.

THE UNDERSTANDING CLAUSE

Mississippi state constitution, which had been written in 1868, remained in effect as written for more than twenty-two years. In 1873 the legislature had ratified both the Fourteenth and Fifteenth amendments. However, between 1875 and 1890, the Mississippi Democratic party did everything within its power to keep blacks from voting. Mississippi became the first state to completely ignore the Fifteenth Amendment. In 1890 the Mississippi Constitutional Convention made the payment of a poll tax (two dollars) required of all voters.[30]

Many of the Democrats believed that a poll tax alone was not enough to keep blacks from voting. Therefore, a state senator, James Z. George, submitted the "understanding clause" for ratification. This clause required that no one be permitted to register or to vote, even if registered, unless he could read and write, or unless he could understand a section of the state constitution, when read to him, and give a reasonable interpretation of it.

The requirement of "reasonable understanding" placed all power in the hands of the registrars or election officials. They decided who had given a reasonable answer to questions of their own devising. And they decided who could and could not vote.[31]

A substitute plan requiring educational qualifications for voting, which would apply to all, was considered. Many speeches were made in favor of both proposals. The most informative speech was given by one speaker in favor of the understanding clause: "If you fail in the discharge of your duties in this matter . . . the blood of every Negro that will be killed in an election riot hereafter will be upon your shoulders."[32]

With the rise of the Democratic party, riots and killings had been taking place, making Mississippi a lawless, corrupted state. Some believed that the Democratic party could increase its power without all the bloodshed if the understanding clause passed. "If the Negro was disenfranchised according to the forms of law, there would be no . . . occasion to suppress his vote by violence because he would have no vote to suppress; and there would be no occasion to commit fraud in the count or perjury in the returns."[33] This was a plea for blacks to give up their voting rights to save white Mississippians from moral corruption!

The Republicans seemed to have enough votes to defeat the understanding clause. There was only one African-American delegate attending the constitutional convention, Isaiah T. Montgomery, from Bolivar County. He was the son of Benjamin Thornton Montgomery, who had been a slave plantation manager for Jefferson Davis. Everyone was shocked when he announced that he planned to make a speech in support of the understanding clause and to vote for it. His was the deciding vote.

Why? Lynch was puzzled. "Why this man, who had the reputation of being honest and honorable and who in point of intelligence was considerably above average of his race should have thus acted and voted has always been an inexplicable mystery."[34]

Possibly Montgomery felt, as did Booker T. Washington, who was active in Alabama at the time, that if blacks stopped creating dissension among whites about suffrage and prepared themselves for citizenship through self-help and education, they would progress more rapidly. Montgomery seemed to see the understanding clause as a means of helping both blacks and poor whites become better citizens by understanding the foundation of their government, the state constitution.

Of course, this reasoning, which Montgomery later admitted privately was false, gained him favors. Like Booker T., who announced his idea that blacks and whites could be in "all things purely social as separate as the fingers," Montgomery became an accommodationist. That was the term for one who believed that accepting limited political activity and concentrating on self-help and industrial education would bring the greatest returns. Both Montgomery and Washington were popular among whites in the South.

The people of Mississippi never had a chance to vote on this 1890 constitution. Members of the convention, the majority of them Democrats, simply declared it in effect as written.[35]

Those who believed that blacks were meant to be servants, "the hewers of wood and drawers of water," were dominant. The fertile fields of Mississippi were white with cotton, and black hands picked it under miserable conditions, for pitiful wages.

Here is Du Bois's conclusion about Reconstruction politics:

> Negro suffrage failed because it was overthrown by brute force. Even if it had been the best government on earth, force, exercised by a majority of richer, more intelligent and more experienced men, could have overthrown it. . . .The South proved by appropriate propaganda that Negro government was the worst ever seen and that it threatened civilization. They suited their propaganda to their audience. They had tried the accusation of laziness but that was refuted by a restoration of agriculture to the prewar level and beyond it. They tried the accusation of ignorance but this was answered by the Negro schools.[36]

Racism had won. Racism is a belief in the superiority of one race over another. A racist is one who creates institutions and laws to make that belief a reality. What if the good white people of Mississippi and the might of the United States government had stood up to the racists of Mississippi after slavery? But they didn't. When a brutal lynching occurred, they looked the other way. When black families were forced off their land and denied decent wages, whites were blind to their plight. A system of apartheid was established.

Mississippi and the South lost the chance to prove that a democratic system that meets the needs of all of the people, regardless of race, can make a dynamic society. Dr. Du Bois summed up the tragedy of that period:

> God wept; but that mattered little to an unbelieving age; what mattered most was that the world wept and still is weeping and blind with tears and blood.[37]

The ground was plowed and made ready for the seeds of the Challenge.

Black folks plant the cotton
Black folks pick it out
White man pockets the money
Black folks do without.
—*Field hand's song*

I'm so tired of such conditions
that I sometimes think life for
me ain't worthwhile.
—*Anonymous*

I'm tired of this jimcrow,
Gonna leave this jimcrow town.
—*Mississippi blues*

6. *MANY THOUSAND GONE*

*B*y the time the Student Nonviolent Coordinating Committee (SNCC) began its work in Mississippi, the state had successfully executed two plans that greatly affected the black population. First, with blacks lacking the power to vote, the state had achieved complete solidification of a one-party system (Democratic). And second, it had achieved depopulation of blacks, insuring the white majority necessary to maintain political power in most counties.

In a state where the majority population initially was black, drastic measures were needed to realize those goals. The suppression and repression began in 1875, with the tacit approval of the U.S. Congress and the U.S. Supreme Court. Three specific rulings of the Court granted Mississippi states' rights, which it used to reduce African Americans to a status only slightly above that of slavery.

(1) The issue of states' rights came up in 1873, when Louisiana courts granted one slaughterhouse control over the slaughtering business. Other, smaller houses filed suit against the state under the Fourteenth Amendment, contending that the monopoly deprived them of property without due process of law. The Supreme Court ruled in favor of the state of Louisiana, declaring that the Fourteenth Amendment applied *only* to African Americans. In other words, a state had jurisdiction over the rights of its citizens. This ruling greatly diminished the civil rights of all citizens in all states, especially the rights of African Americans in the state of Mississippi.

(2) In 1896 the Court ruled, in the case of *Plessey v. Ferguson*, that "separate but equal" public facilities for blacks and whites were within the law.

(3) In 1898, a third decision was made, concerning a Mississippi black named Henry Williams, who had been indicted by an all-white grand jury and sentenced for murder by an all-white jury. His counsel appealed to the Supreme Court, arguing that Williams had been denied equal protection under the law because the 1890 constitution made it impossible for blacks to vote. Because they could not vote, they could not qualify to serve as jurors. The Court ruled in favor of Mississippi,

pointing out that constitutions and statutes

> do not on their face discriminate between the races, and
> it has not been shown that the actual administration was
> evil; only that evil was possible under them.[1]

In effect, the Court gave approval to the design of the Mississippi constitution to disenfranchise blacks.

Blacks continued to see their rights eroded. As early as 1903, a labor force of sharecroppers, tenant farmers, and field hands was working under conditions slightly above those of slavery. Only now the former masters were not responsible for the necessities of life or the burial of their workers. The educational system that northern whites and freedmen had turned over to the state, the first public school system in the history of Mississippi, set standards that were the lowest in the nation.

When James K. Vardaman ran for governor in 1903, a Mississippi-born scholar, James Wilford Garner, was appalled by the candidate's hatred. He described the campaign as "one without precedent for low-down vulgarity and indecency. There can be no doubt that the hostility of the whites to the blacks is increasing."[2]

This hostility manifested itself in the use of state and federal funds to keep blacks ignorant, docile, and dependent. They were not allowed to purchase or own land, or to vote.

The Reverend Charles B. Galloway, bishop of the Methodist Church South, seeing the rise of the Ku Klux Klan and other racist groups, spoke of a "measure of despair [and] great unrest . . . among negroes. They are

Black children were forced to attend school in churches, lodge halls, and other buildings that could not, by law, receive school funds.

John E. Phay Collection
University of Mississippi

beginning to feel friendless and hopeless."

JIM CROW: SEPARATE BUT NOT EQUAL

In 1899 Mississippi superintendent of education A. A. Kincannon had stated, "Our public school system is designed primarily for the welfare of the white children of the state, and incidentally for the negro children."[3]

In the 1900s, blacks made up 60 percent of the school population, yet they received only 19 percent of the state's school funds. In 1930 the yearly figures were $33.31 per white student and $5.94 per black student.[4]

Most black schools for children below fifth grade were housed in churches and lodge rooms. They had only one teacher. In some counties, schools had been built by the white philanthropist Julius Rosenwald. In 1924 the amount of money spent on schools supported by the Rosenwald Fund was more than a million dollars. Much of that, $445,357, was contributed by blacks. Even though these schools were built by the Rosenwald Fund, the state still refused to equip them.

By the mid-1930s, the average black school in southern states was valued at $36 per black pupil, compared to $183 per white.

In Mississippi the valuation was $11 to $147, a ratio of $1 for whites to 7¢ for blacks.

The state often gave blacks the shell of a building, which they had to finish themselves. With few skilled workers in the rural areas, and no funds for building supplies, these schools met no standards for comfort or safety.

While buses and taxis were used to transport whites

to comfortably built schools, blacks walked miles in cold rain, or on ice-hardened roads, to dilapidated, one-room buildings that often leaked and had inadequate heating and no sanitary facilities.

One schoolmaster, describing his school, said:

> It was little better than teaching out of doors. When it rained the water came through the top, but through the sides as well. The little fellows would be standing in water below like little ducks. . . . Many of them were not protected with overshoes or any shoes, but they came to school each day much as if they were properly clad.[5]

Children often went to school at the risk of their families being turned off the land. Every hand within a family was needed to chop, weed, and pick cotton.

William Holtzclaw, who became a dedicated teacher in Mississippi, often raised funds in northern cities for his school. In Neil McMillen's *Dark Journey*, Professor Holtzclaw, who was educated in the state, tells of the risks his mother took to keep him in school:

> "When the landlord came to the quarters early in the morning to stir up cotton pickers, she used to outgeneral him by hiding me behind the skillets, ovens and pots, throwing some old rags over me until he was gone." Then after slipping him off to school through the woods and underbrush, "she joined the other pickers in the field working at double-time to make up to the landlord for the work of us both. . . ." At the age of nine [his] education was continued on alternate days, his brother going to school one day, he the next. "What he learned on his school day, he taught me at night. I did the same for him."[6]

Some black children did not go to school at all. Some went only to the fourth grade. Besides being needed at home to work in the fields, children had to have books, supplies, and clothing. These were luxury items. One teacher explained:

> If you went to school, you went after Christmas . . . because the cotton had been harvested and you had money to buy clothes. When there were hard times, many children didn't go at all; didn't have nothin' fittin' to wear.[7]

Parents and teachers worked hard to keep what schools they had. Some of these schools planted their own cotton, cultivated gardens, and kept dairy herds. A few even had sawmills. But most depended upon private funds received from outside the South. Some schools sent singers throughout the United States and abroad to raise needed funds. Communities held bake sales, taffy pulls, musicals, and other projects to raise money. Some parents sent baskets of eggs, garden produce, and painfully written letters: "dear 'fesser please 'cept dis 18 cents it is all I has save it out n my washing dis week god will bless you will send some more next week."[8]

As late as 1945, many of Mississippi's black schools were mere shells with no equipment, no running water, and no outhouses. Most of the schools were still housed in churches, lodge rooms, and other nonpublic build- ings that did not qualify under the law for public funds to make improvements. Even whites admitted that many a school was unfit even for cotton storage: "hardly better than cow sheds," "fire traps, with temperatures below

Entire families of sharecroppers worked in the fields, yet they often stayed indebted to the landowners for years.

The Bettman Archive

freezing." Where there were maps, erasers, and fuel, these were supplied by private funds. Only about 5 percent had library books, and those were not "related to the children's needs."[9]

In 1945, the salaries of black teachers were cruelly inadequate; $33 a month, less than a fourth of the $150 per month earned by white teachers. The salaries of black administrators were as bad or worse. It was estimated that one-fourth of the teachers left their jobs each year, unable to live off the small salaries.

The rare whites, such as state superintendent Willard F. Bond, who thought that the black child, if educated, could become "a valuable asset," also felt that blacks should still be taught as a people meant to be docile, dependent manual laborers.

Many whites thought that since few blacks owned land, their share of taxes was insignificant. They did not understand that taxes were levied on more than land. Black sharecroppers and tenant farmers paid rent to help landlords pay taxes; blacks paid excise taxes and civil and criminal fines. Revenues came from the forced labor of prisoners, who were mostly black. The amount of this revenue was often considerable. Blacks understood the tax base and the fact that their taxes were being used to educate white children, while their children were educationally deprived.

PARENTS AND TEACHERS ORGANIZE

With the state starving black children educationally and black teachers financially, just how did black parents seek to educate their children? Teachers had formed the Mississippi Association of Teachers in Colored Schools as early as 1906, and parents organized the Mississippi Congress of Colored Parents and Teachers in 1926. As blacks have done since emancipation, these parents and teachers sought relief in the courts. They petitioned the legislators to separate school funds the way they had separated their schools. Let the taxes that blacks paid go directly into funds for black schools. The legislators refused. Parents were struggling against such people as former Governor Bilbo, who edited the newspaper *Free Lance*:

> A certain bunch of Negroes in Mississippi very boldly and brazenly carried to the Mississippi legislature a petition setting out their claims, rights and demands. Some of these demands were so out of harmony with a white man's country and a white man's government that a few years ago if such a thing had been attempted they would have been bodily thrown out of the halls. . . .[10]

Some sharecroppers and tenant farmers solved their problems by leaving areas where landowners refused to build schools. Others used their labor as a bargaining tool for their children's education. In a few Mississippi counties, and in the all-black town of Mound Bayou, blacks built their own schools.

Around 1925, in Mount Olive, blacks called upon county supervisors, who had levied a school tax on both whites and blacks, to levy a second and separate tax on their property, to be used for black schools. Keep in mind that these were relatively poor people, only sixty years out of slavery. They had no power. They had only the burning desire to educate their children. A second tax was levied and a black school was built in Mount Olive. Blacks continued to bear the burden of educating white children.

THE EARTH IS THE LANDLORD'S

Many of the Africans enslaved in Mississippi had lived off the land in West Africa. In the United States they knew nothing but tilling the soil. It was, therefore, natural that, when emancipated, they wanted to continue working on farms. But they also wanted the independence that comes only with property. The unkept promise of land to African Americans for their assistance to the Union in the Civil War affected their outlook and adjustment to freedom. The desire and pressure for promised land died slowly, as many continued to hold out against signing contracts for their labor.

Well after the Confederates had been pardoned and had reclaimed the land that had been allotted to African Americans during Reconstruction, most blacks finally gave up hope of becoming property owners. They then began to sign contracts to work on other men's land. The contracts set forth how long they would work and whether they would sharecrop or become tenants.

In one way or another, some became small-farm owners, operating on a shoestring, with little to show for their work except proud ownership. Others, with the help of planters, purchased larger tracts of land. Many who owned such tracts, however, were mulattoes whose white relatives granted them acreage. This was perhaps true of such African Americans as Benjamin T.

67

Montgomery, who leased a four-thousand-acre plantation from his former master, Jefferson Davis, and then
later purchased the land. He was said to be "the best
planter in the county and perhaps in the state." His
cotton won all the prizes at the Cincinnati Exposition
in 1873.[11]

When Benjamin Montgomery died in 1878, his land
went to his son, Isaiah (the same Isaiah Montgomery
who gave the deciding vote for the understanding
clause). Later Isaiah had difficulty with the Davis heirs
and was forced to leave the land. He settled in Bolivar
County and, with other blacks from the plantation,
founded Mound Bayou.

Most blacks, unlike mulattoes, were not readily
given the opportunity to purchase land. This was especially true for those who sought acreage in the rich bottom lands of the rivers. They were permitted to buy
land in counties where the majority were not blacks—
the hilly, infertile piney woods. Unable to obtain capital
and with no credit, they acquired the poorest plots; and
they often paid much more per acre for these than did
whites. As late as 1934, a federal study discovered that
"it is often true that the negro settles as a farm owner on
land that the white people cannot afford to cultivate."[12]

Nevertheless, in the ten years between 1890 and
1900, black landownership almost doubled. Then, from
1900 on, it declined. This decline was due to many
factors: White banks refused to lend or give credit;
black banks did not thrive very long in the state;
the cost of land to blacks, even the poorest of land, was
much more than what whites paid; and white violence

from the Ku Klux Klan was out of control.

Dirt farmers, especially those in the hilly pines area (Cane Hill Billies), formed terrorist groups and called themselves the White Caps. White Caps often burned the barns, homes, and crops of blacks, with no fear of being punished. Those blacks most likely to be targets were the most industrious and prosperous. Docile blacks who sought to "elevate themselves morally" were promised White Cap protection. Those who sought education and independence were ordered out of some counties. In 1902, whites in Amite County posted signs on blacks' land, informing them:

> If you have not moved away from here by sundown tomorrow, we will shoot you like rabbits. All negroes out of this county.[13]

More than a dozen blacks were murdered, and scores were beaten and driven from their farms. Even whites began to fear the "destruction of all legal government and the enthronement of naked brute force as the governing power in the community."[14] One white churchman declared, "Unless conditions are radically changed . . . our cotton will lie fallow. Already the scarcity of labor is the despair of large landowners."[14]

Blacks fled Mississippi in great numbers, leaving banks unable to collect debts, businesses in bad economic straits, and farm landowners without tenants. Now that the economy had been hit, White Caps were arrested. Some were sentenced to life imprisonment but were immediately pardoned. Three hundred received suspended sentences in federal courts, for intimidating black homesteaders.[15] Finally, in 1906, lawlessness in some counties ended. Whites understood that as much as they wanted blacks to leave the state, they needed them as laborers and consumers.

By 1930, in counties of the rich Yazoo Delta, about 74 percent of the population was black, but only 2.3 percent of these blacks owned their land. Blacks in Mound Bayou owned more farmland than any other blacks in the delta. Still, whites owned 90 percent of all farmland in that county, and 98.2 percent of all black farmers were tenants.[16]

In the period immediately following Reconstruction, a few blacks were permitted to prosper: As in all oppressive systems, there have to be some successes to keep the masses hopeful. At every gathering of the Mississippi Negro Farmers or the Mississippi Negro Business League, these success stories were told over and over to spur the ordinary farmers to keep their eyes on the prize. Professor Holtzclaw constantly reminded the landless that "Mississippi's black landowner was the backbone of our beloved commonwealth. . . . You must not get discouraged in your efforts. You must buy land. . . . Every honest effort will bear fruit."[17]

For the industrious, and for those lucky enough to have a white friend or relative, that encouragement sometimes worked. And, too, in places where blacks were able to organize and help farmers, the chances of them becoming landowners greatly increased. Holtzclaw formed the Black Belt Improvement Society. By 1930, the society had created a colony of blacks who owned several thousand acres of land near the school he ran.

Ninety-five percent of the people in the area owned their homes and farms. This was, however, only a very small percentage of the land in Mississippi.

In good times, African Americans bought farms, paying fifty dollars an acre for land that a white had purchased for only ten dollars an acre. Then, in bad times, when debts could not be paid, the landlord fore-closed, making far more than he would have made if he had hired the black farmers as tenants. He was now free to resell. People who were so desirous of land often became prey to white owners. Neil McMillen in *Dark Journey* records one African American: "They'll get their money, and yet find ways to keep the title to the land. So Negroes got wary, and won't try to buy land."[6]

Many who worked hard and kept their livestock, barns, and homes in good shape were targets of jealous whites. They were the ones most likely to be burned out, or to have their tools and livestock stolen. Blacks soon learned they had to do either one of two things: keep their property in terrible condition, or pretend igno-rance and docility. They had to "yes sir" the "master." This became a strategy for survival, but it enabled whites to look upon blacks as lazy and careless, with no desire to achieve.

During times of natural disasters, such as the arrival of the boll weevil, that little insect that devours cotton, or floods and droughts, and during economic depressions, many blacks never recovered. These crises, along with racial discrimination, left people without hope.

The federal government recognized the needs of small farmers and made efforts to provide them some relief. Black farmers in Mississippi rarely benefited from these grants. Just as whites had used all the state taxes for their own programs, they used all but meager amounts of federal farming money for their own needs. The Smith-Lever Act (1914), providing agricultural and home demonstrations, was intended to serve blacks and whites equally.

Agricultural demonstration agents helped farmers plan crops, conserve the soil, and produce bigger harvests and healthier animals. Home demonstration agents helped families improve their health and nutrition by teaching better methods of canning, drying, and smoking to preserve food. Mississippi senator and former governor James K. Vardaman blocked the provision in the bill that granted an equal share of monies to blacks and whites. Therefore, white agricultural and home demonstration agents were paid out of federal funds, while those few blacks who were hired were paid out of second taxes from the black community.

In Mississippi counties where black demonstration agents were finally paid by government funds, the agents did not spend their time working with black farmers to improve their skills. Instead they spent their time as described by a county extension-service report revealed in 1946:

> The Negro county agent was called on by many landlords to assist in finding cooks, drivers, yard boys and other help around the farm home. . . . Not one Negro farmer in a hundred had ever seen a county agent, the black extension worker's principal job was to do chores—to vaccinate livestock, tend orchards, and service machin-

Sharecroppers and tenant farmers were forced to use whatever materials they could find to repair their homes and schools.

The Bettman Archive

ery—not for Negro farmers, but for the well-to-do white farmers, who least needed assistance, but whose opinions carry weight with county politicians.[18]

Black farm families continued to hire themselves out in one of two capacities: as tenants (renting land and working it in ways they thought best), or as sharecroppers. Tenant farmers had to have capital to purchase livestock, tools, seeds, and fertilizer. Therefore they were a little more independent than sharecroppers, who relied upon the landowner to supply all of their needs, including food and clothing, usually from a commissary on the land.

Many still worked from "can't to can't," and often at the end of the cotton season, many had nothing to show for their work but debt to the landowner. For meager supplies purchased on credit at the landowner's commissary, they paid interest rates of between 20 and 60 percent. Many sank deeper and deeper into debt, with no way out unless another farmer moved them onto his farm, debt included. The cycle was begun again, with just enough hope to think "maybe next year."

One African American described the plight of the average field hand in 1930:

> Pitiable, pitiable! You can't know what they have to take.... You can't imagine.... The South won the war.... Poor devils are just the same as his slaves. Now they have him still in economic slavery and they don't have to feed or clothe him or pay a doctor when he's sick.[19]

In 1972 former tenant farmers were asked to remember pre–World War II conditions on plantations. One, Clara Hampton, said,

> At that time the peoples whupped you here, and they [blacks] are still afraid to come here[,] still think that's going on now.[20]

There were others who preferred to talk about how some blacks did not take beatings and faced "the man" with threats of retaliation. Robert Allen remembered and told of his experience.

> None never did beat me, 'cause I told um, I say, "you won't beat me, you might kill me, but you won't never beat."[21]

He recalled the time his father stood his ground against a white man:

> "I'll give you some of it," [the white man threatened] and he [the elder Allen] said, "naw you won't." He say "you won't come out like you think you will." Well he let him by. . . . That was my daddy. My daddy didn't stand for that. He, he wuz fullah African and . . . they didn't fool wid him.[22]

WHITE DEATH

The plan to undereducate, render landless, and force many blacks out of the state worked. Still, a reign of terror against blacks continued. Though this terror was constant, there were periods when it became more frenetic—from 1889 to 1908, and from 1918 to 1922, just after World War I. The most common form of terror came from the shocking mob lynchings that blacks called the "white death." From 1889 to 1903 there were more than 88 lynchings in Mississippi; between 1904 and 1908 there were 74, an average of one every twenty-five days.[23]

The total number of lynchings up through the 1930s in Mississippi, 476 (some records state 600), was 13 percent of all lynchings in the United States (3,724). Texas and Georgia had a great number of lynchings, too, but Mississippi ranked first in every category:

> total lynchings; multiple lynchings; most per capita; the most female victims (1 white, 14 black with 2 being in an advanced state of pregnancy); the most victims taken from police custody; lynchings without arrest or conviction of mob leaders; and the most public support for vigilantism.[24]

Before 1900, mob violence against African Americans usually took the form of shootings and hangings. But between 1900 and 1940, an even more barbarous type of "white death" became common: mutilation and burning. During this period,

> at least 15 blacks died in public burnings, a method described by one newspaper as NEGRO BARBE-CUES. . . . In some instances the agony of the victims was reported in graphic detail by white journalists apparently eager to satisfy the public appetite for gore. . . . Before Luther Holbert and his wife were burned by whites who charged them with murdering a planter, the Vicksburg *Evening Post* noted, "they suffered the most fiendish tortures" by hands of whites who chopped off their fingers and ears one by one, gouged their eyes until they "hung by a shred from their socket," and

pulled "big pieces of raw, quivering flesh" from their bodies with corkscrews. A crowd estimated at one thousand observed the butchery.[25]

A black guilty of such affronts as "insubordination," "talking disrespectfully," "striking a white man," "slapping a white boy," "a personal debt of fifty cents," "an unpaid funeral bill of ten dollars," being "too prosperous," "conjuring," and "mistaken identity" could be burned to death or mutilated. In the minds of most white Mississippians this savagery fell into two categories: a good lynching or a bad lynching. A good lynching was one in which "a relatively few disciplined whites swiftly executed a 'bad niggah' charged with a heinous crime." A bad lynching "featured a surfeit of liquor and firearms and an unruly, indiscriminate mob that threatened the peace and dignity of an entire community. . . . A bad lynching means a burning."[26]

While governor, James K. Vardaman declared; "If it is necessary every Negro in the state will be lynched; it will be done to maintain white supremacy."[27]

Why such an attitude against blacks, which caused such drastic measures for what seemed such trivial matters? Some whites, such as James Street, a Mississippi writer who at fourteen covered his first lynching as a cub reporter, seek to place blame on poor whites who needed to punish blacks to affirm their solidarity with the white upper class and maintain the white caste system: "The lynching citizenry [was] the ignorant, hot-blooded trash, the leavings [of] the poolrooms and log cabins."[28]

Why was there no outcry by law-abiding, decent white Mississippians against such crimes? Blacks felt that this brutal treatment persisted out of sheer hatred and because all whites, regardless of class, shared in that communal ritual of bloody burning. However, John Dollard, in *Caste and Class in a Southern Town*, says: "In the end it seems a better statement to say that white people fear Negroes. . . . This fear, of course, has a long history, fear of revolt, fear of Negroes' running away, and fear of isolated assault or terrorism."[29]

It has been said that fear is the mother of hatred, but the kind of irrational, brutal torture that occurred in the early and middle twentieth century defies defense. White men who were asked about lynchings talked about rape. Many felt what Neil McMillen quotes Vardaman as saying: "Mob violence in some form . . . was often the only 'adequate punishment' for a black 'two-legged monster' who defiled 'the exalted virtue, the vestal purity and superlative qualities of southern woman.' "[30] Yet, out of 3,724 lynchings committed from 1889 through 1930, more than four-fifths of the dead were blacks, and of those, less than one-sixth were even accused of rape.

Regardless of the reasons, it is safe to say that the threat of "white death" was ever present in the minds of black people, and especially black males as late as 1960. This fear remains and is often remembered years later. One black told of an incident that happened when he was eight years old:

A Negro came panting up to the house one day, his shirt open and his body dripping with sweat. He asked for a drink of water . . . which was given to him from the well. Instead of leaving by the front gate, the man leaped over the back fence and ran away across the fields. In about fifteen minutes a group of white men came up to the house and asked if they had seen a Negro run by. . . . The father had come in the meantime and told the posse he had seen no one. The boy did not mention the water. The white party went on. In a few minutes [the] informant heard plainly the dull thud of guns. He learned later that the Negro had been killed.[31]

There are many such stories. Richard Wright, the novelist noted for *Native Son*, stated:

A dread of white people came to live permanently in my imagination. I had already grown to feel that there existed men against whom I was powerless, men who could violate my life at will. . . . There did not exist to my knowledge any possible course of action which could have saved me if I had ever been confronted with a white mob.[32]

Good citizens averted their eyes. Law-enforcement officers, if not actually involved, did nothing to prevent seizure of jailed suspects, and no mob leader is known to have been punished. Police officials refused to launch investigations when ordered to do so. Some victims were seized in daylight hours and blowtorched immediately after their trials for murder. Yet no one was able to identify the mob leaders.

White newspapers aided and abetted lynchers, advertising and praising their tactics, looking upon them as men who expressed the will of the people. Churches avoided social issues, sticking strictly to personal matters of piety and morals. No minister dared offend members who might be part of mobs.[33]

There was one Mississippi governor, Andrew H. Longino, who in 1899 tried to curb the violence. He offered compensation to families of lynch victims and wanted to dismiss peace officers who failed to protect their charges. Nothing came of his suggestions, and he did not pursue them. Nevertheless, when he sought election for a second term, the people of Mississippi remembered his efforts and voted him out.

Governor Vardaman, the most adamant white supremacist, once used the militia to prevent a double lynching and was accused of going against the wishes of "every white man in the state."[34] It is also reported that Governor Dennis Murphee lost the governorship to Theodore Bilbo because he used the Mississippi National Guard to prevent a lynching.

During Governor Bilbo's tenure, announcements were made in the Jackson *Daily News* and, across state lines, in the New Orleans *State*, for the lynching of John Hartfield:

> 3,000 WILL BURN NEGRO
> JOHN HARTFIELD LYNCHED BY ELLISVILLE MOB
> AT 5 O'CLOCK THIS AFTERNOON
> NEGRO JERKY AND SULLEN AS BURNING HOUR NEARS

Afterward the paper reported:

> At the appointed hour, the black was kicked unconscious, hanged from an ancient sycamore tree, and riddled with bullets before his body was engulfed by flames.[35]

80

Governor Bilbo claimed he was "powerless to prevent" this well-advertised event. He acted on his belief that "this is strictly a white man's country . . . and any dream on the part of the Negro race to share social and political equality will be shattered in the end." [36]

The only recourse blacks had was to flee. Some moved into neighboring southern states, others fled north. This was part of the Mississippi plan. However, when so many left that the Mississippi economy again suffered from the lack of black consumers and workers, great efforts were made to stop the wave of departures. Blacks were forcibly taken out of cars and off of buses and trains. Rumors were spread about blacks starving and freezing to death in the North. Blacks still took the risk of leaving. From 1910 to 1960, it is estimated that almost one million (938,000) blacks fled the state. [37]

Finally, in the early thirties, Mississippi white women, possibly having become aware of the disadvantages of bearing the burden of "exalted virtue, vestal purity, and superlative qualities," decided to join other southern women in the national fight against lynch mobs. They joined the Association of Southern Women for the Prevention of Lynching (ASWPL), which had been founded in Atlanta, Georgia, in November of 1930. Led by Bessie C. Alfred of McComb and Ethel Featherstun Stevens of Jackson, Mississippi women pursued a program of education through community forums and antilynching institutes. They privately investigated lynchings, and pressed state officials for law and order.

During all this time, from 1892 on, Ida B. Wells, a

black woman, had been waging a crusade against lynching. Although born in Mississippi in 1869, she lived in Tennessee, where she taught school and published a small newspaper, the Memphis *Free Speech*. Her paper circulated throughout the Yazoo Delta. When it exposed the lynching of three young black businessmen in Memphis, her office was destroyed, and she was forced to leave the South. She settled in Chicago. There she documented the number of lynchings in the United States and crusaded at home and abroad for the prevention of the violent deaths. It was she who first contended and proved statistically that the "protection of white womanhood" was not the reason for so many lynchings. Instead, mob violence was used to intimidate blacks to keep them on the plantations and to prevent them from voting.

Ida B. Wells worked with the NAACP, which spent a sizable amount of its small resources trying to curb lynchings in Mississippi. However, investigations and exposures of senseless violence came to naught. In 1939, the NAACP organizers felt the futility of their efforts and declared that "beyond publicity . . . there is nothing we can do in Mississippi courts. Our only hope is through continued efforts for passage of the federal antilynching law."[38] Hope for such federal assistance was bashed, as most hope for blacks had been since 1883, when the liberal Democratic president, Franklin Delano Roosevelt, failed to support an antilynching law in 1934, and a civil rights act in 1935.

The lynchings continued. White women in Mississippi stepped up their actions. They appealed to the

Methodist churches and the Mississippi Baptist Convention but received no support. They were attacked in the press as being afflicted by a "Negro complex." Finally, in 1936, the Methodist church adopted its first anti-lynching resolution.[39]

ASWPL members in Mississippi, along with others, such as Lillian Smith of Georgia, who wrote the novel *Strange Fruit*, describing the horrors of lynching, and Billie Holiday, the black singer, who sang a song of the same title, unearthed the loathing of people for such crimes. From 1939 to 1945, the NAACP reported twenty-seven lynchings in the United States, of which six were said to have occurred in Mississippi. Gradually, the tide of "white death," in the form of burning and mutilation, confronted by adverse public opinion, receded.

WORLD WAR II AND HUMAN RIGHTS

The beginning of World War II, in 1939, created a climate in which ideas about human rights for people outside of the United States exposed the denial of those rights at home. The government encouraged people to fight for freedom against tyranny and oppression.

In the preparation for the war, many opportunities opened up for blacks in the building of warships, warplanes, and other necessary equipment.

Many blacks left Mississippi, not only for the North, but for the West: California, Oregon, and the state of Washington. Because of the wartime economy, they fared much better than did those who had fled in 1920. Still, there were many who stayed. And those who did

These soldiers were part of the all-black 92nd Division, which fought to protect democracy and human rights during World War II.

UPI/Bettman

realized that the practice of denying them quality education, decent housing, and jobs with equal pay was not over. Nor was the threat of death. True, there were not the blatant burnings and mutilations. The deaths came in more subtle forms but were just as great in numbers.

At the end of World War II, African-American veterans returned to Mississippi. They had fought to rid the world of Hitler and had a new will to end oppression at home. They talked about what they had seen in the world and about what they had done. Those blacks who had stayed in Mississippi, waging a struggle against impossible odds, listened.

But after the war, blacks still disappeared, and no one was able to account for just how many were murdered. In 1959, Mack Charles Parker was openly lynched. The murders committed throughout the 1960s fitted this description: "[The victims'] disappearance is shrouded in mystery, for they are dispatched quickly and without general knowledge. In some lonely swamp a small body of men do the job formerly done by a vast, howling, blood-thirsty mob."[40]

Part Two

Got one mind for white folks to see
'Nother for what I know is me
They don't know,
They don't know my mind.
—*Mississippi blues*

7. FREEDOM—A CONSTANT SORROW

Mississippians saw and felt the stirrings for freedom of blacks nationwide, but their struggle in the form of direct action did not start in the fifties, as it did in some other southern states with less harsh and brutal histories. There were few national black organizations in the state to create and support action for change.

Approximately five hundred blacks in Mississippi may have belonged to the United Negro Improvement Association (UNIA), founded by Marcus Garvey in 1914. Garvey espoused black pride, self-help, moral uplift, and a return to Africa. All of these ideas had appeal to black Mississippians. Certainly many of them must have longed for a new beginning, and why not in Africa?

UNIA did not cause whites concern. The movement that advocated separateness met with white approval, except for UNIA's "back to Africa" plan, which white Mississippians knew would deprive them of cheap labor.

The NAACP, on the other hand, provoked much opposition from whites. Several times between 1920 and 1945, the NAACP tried to organize branches in Mississippi, but failed each time. With the NAACP in mind, the state legislature passed a law (in 1920) prohibiting the circulation of materials that would cause problems between the races.

Nevertheless, blacks in the middle class, who were not dependent upon whites for their economic well-being, did belong to the NAACP: ministers, doctors, lawyers, health professionals, and businessmen. These were small in number, for at that time most blacks were field hands, domestic servants, or manual laborers. Most lived in rural areas and hardly made enough money to spare for other than bare necessities. And, too, membership remained small because the Klan was still active, and fear of devastating reprisals was rampant.

Any mail from the national NAACP office to members arrived without a return address and was signed with an assumed name. A Vicksburg, Mississippi, member as late as 1939 informed the national office, "I takes a chance whenever I write, they will open my mail going and coming."[1]

There were local organizations, such as the Federation of Colored Women's Clubs and the Committee of One Hundred, that were made up of prominent men and women, many of whom were college graduates. With great subtlety and backdoor diplomacy, they were able to get whites to provide better social services, such as libraries, and to allow African-American history courses in black schools.

They did not petition legislators or create any activities that required direct confrontation. Their main tactics were moral persuasion and negotiation with approachable whites, such as ministers, civic leaders, and businessmen. Somewhat like UNIA, they espoused self-help, moral uplift, and black pride, and they did not face hostility from whites.

In spite of what appeared to be resignation to the status quo and an unwillingness to try to make changes through direct action, in 1940 the Committee of One Hundred merged with the NAACP. Many of the committee's members, unknown to whites, were already members of the national organization. They had come to understand that changes taking place in the country and in the world made it possible for them to become more active and to try other tactics. However, their strategies were not in any way similar to those used by blacks in states where the treatment was less harsh.

There are no known efforts of blacks in Mississippi to integrate public places, other than a boycott of public transportation in 1904. Under Governor Vardaman, a law was passed that decreed separate trolley cars or separate compartments within trolley cars for black and white riders. Blacks in cities boycotted the trolley, and

91

because they made up 40 to 50 percent of the ridership, they were almost successful. However, the power of blacks at that time was so limited that, with no support from the courts, the effort finally failed.[2]

Failure was followed by inactivity and accommodation, because of the hostility of whites. However, some historians believe this lack of activity for integration was divided between necessity and a "matter of pride and preference." Having early established their own churches, lodges, and other places for social gatherings, blacks found a self-identity that made them basically satisfied with their autonomous relations with whites. But they wanted equal education and equal political rights, which in turn would guarantee equal economic status. In 1920 C. E. Johnson, an agriculture demonstration agent, declared, "We want only one thing, primarily. That is the ballot."[3]

In 1950, inspired by young blacks home from the war, blacks in the Delta came together and organized the Regional Council of Negro Leadership at an elementary school in Cleveland, Mississippi. In May of that year, some thirteen thousand people from forty countries assembled at Mound Bayou. At that meeting, the goals of the council were established: to teach blacks first-class citizenship and to insure that blacks learned how to calculate taxes, how to get and hold office, how to preserve their property, and how to change their economic status.[4]

In 1954, the Supreme Court decision in the *Brown v. Board of Education of Topeka* case on school desegregation overturned the *Plessey v. Ferguson* decision of 1896, bringing hope. Maybe after more than half a century, the highest Court of the land was willing to reverse itself and interpret laws supporting the Fourteenth Amendment that blacks should have equal protection and equal opportunities, and that separate facilities were inherently unequal. States were required to integrate their public schools "with all deliberate speed."

On May 7, 1955, Aaron Henry, a pharmacist and a leader in the NAACP, organized the Council of Federated Organizations (COFO). The council members were educators; community leaders such as Elks, businessmen, ministers; and leaders of the NAACP. COFO came into being as a direct result of the Court order for integration of schools. However, there seemed to be little interest in integration in Mississippi; therefore, the council lay dormant until 1960.

Governor Ross Barnett labeled the leaders of COFO Communists. In October of 1955, in Indianola, Mississippi, the White Citizens Council was organized. Its aim was to resist any changes in the South that might occur because of the Supreme Court ruling. The state, through its Sovereignty Commission, granted the council financial support for its programs, as much as ninety thousand dollars. The council promoted activities that denied blacks work, credit, or a chance to survive.[5]

Also in 1955, Amzie Moore, a postal worker and gas-station owner and a native of Grenada, Mississippi, was elected president of the Cleveland branch of the NAACP. Amzie, a World War II veteran, had returned to Mississippi in 1946 at a time when an organization known as the home guard was terrorizing blacks. The guard had been formed especially to "protect" white families from returning black soldiers. Amzie described the situation: "For about six or eight months at least one negro each week was killed. I think the purpose of the killing was to frighten other negroes. It certainly had its psychological effect."[6]

Those who knew Amzie Moore had great respect for his fearlessness, his courage, and his leadership capabilities. He knew and was in close touch with other NAACP leaders, such as Ella Baker, who would help organize SNCC in 1960, and E. D. Nixon of Montgomery, Alabama, who had initiated the 1955 bus boycott in that city. In a recent conversation, Diane Nash Bevel of SNCC remembered Amzie as a "large built, pleasant, easy-going person. He was a Christian, well educated, and remarkably versed in the Bible."

When Amzie was elected president of the Cleveland branch of the NAACP, there were about eighty-seven members. He recalled how the membership grew rapidly after his election and the consequences of that growth:

> By the middle of the year we had 564 members of that branch. But then we had other things happen in 1955. . . .
>
> On May 7, 1955 about 11:30 at night Mr. George W. Lee was ambushed and killed. Following Mr. Lee's death . . . we had Jack Smith . . . killed at Brookhaven for participating in what they called politics. . . . Then in September, 1955 . . . a boy named Emmett Till. . . . Following the Till case, Gus Coates, a civil rights worker, was shot through the window of his store. . . . After he

was discharged from the hospital, he was advised to leave the state.

Quite a number of leaders left the state: T. R. M. Howard, president of the Regional Council . . . Dr. Battle, of Sunflower county. . . . We had a great exodus of leaders . . . due to the pressure that was being brought on by white organizations bent and bound on maintaining slavery. As 1955 came to a close we found that there had been seven deaths, many people had been hurt, it was a real rough year for Mississippi.[7]

In other parts of the South, exciting things were happening in the fifties, following the *Brown v. Board of Education of Topeka* decision. In Montgomery, Alabama, blacks won their demands in a bus boycott. Nine children were admitted to an all-white high school in Little Rock, Arkansas, and in the same year, 1957, President Eisenhower signed the first civil rights act to pass Congress since 1875. This act made it illegal to interfere with any person's right to vote for any candidate he or she might choose. It further provided that the attorney general of the United States could take action against anyone who tried to deprive any person of voting rights.

After the act became law (1957), Congress authorized the attorney general to bring a suit to prevent denial of the right to vote based on race, color, or national origin.

The NAACP mimeographed hundreds of copies of the Mississippi constitution and set up classes to study it in Mound Bayou under the supervision of Father John Lebouvre. About 150 people were taught that year. Less than 20 passed the voter registration test. By the end of 1957, Father Lebouvre, who was considered a devoted, hardworking priest, was transferred to Pennsylvania. The priest who replaced him decided it was not in the best interest of his church to allow the NAACP to continue voter registration classes in Mound Bayou. The NAACP had to give up its efforts at that time.[10]

Then in April 1960, Congress passed a voting rights act requiring states that interfered with voting rights because of race, color, or national origin to maintain and produce records showing voting and registration patterns.

The Mississippi legislature immediately enacted a law authorizing the destruction of registration records. They also amended the Mississippi constitution to add "good moral character" as a qualification for voting.[8]

That same year, 1960, the Commission on Civil Rights, an independent, bipartisan federal agency established in 1957, began a study of voter registration and voting practices of blacks in Mississippi. The study focused on that state because it had the lowest percentage of black registration.[9]

Estimated Black Voter Registration Percentages in
Southern States in 1956 and 1964

	% 1956	% 1964
Alabama	11	23
Arkansas	36	49.3
Florida	32	63.7
Georgia	27	44
Louisiana	31	32
Mississippi	5	6
North Carolina	24	46.8

South Carolina	27	38.8
Tennessee	29	69.4
Texas	37	57.7
Virginia	19	45.7

The mood in Congress and the new laws encouraged blacks to begin voter-education classes and to make plans to register voters. Mississippi law required every person who registered to fill out a twenty-one-question form and to know 285 sections of the state constitution. People trying to register had to be ready to answer any question asked about the constitution in order to meet the requirements of the understanding clause that had been in effect since 1890. Now they also had to meet the requirements of the new law that required all voters to have "good moral character."

The absolute necessity for blacks to vote—and their desire to do so—remained, in spite of the violence, reprisals, and deaths. With information and specific data and indirect support from the U.S. Justice Department, Amzie Moore resumed planning for a voter registration drive.

That year, 1960, SNCC representative Bob Moses went into Mississippi. Moses, who lived in Harlem, was a mathematics teacher at Horace Mann High School in the Bronx. He went into Mississippi with June Stembridge, a white native of Virginia, who was a secretary in the SNCC office in Atlanta, Georgia. The two were there to recruit participants for a conference SNCC was planning to hold that October in Atlanta.

While in Cleveland, Bob met Amzie. They discussed

African Americans wait to register as white voters walk by.
UPI/Bettman

the plans for voter registration. As were most people who had come into contact with Amzie Moore, Bob was impressed especially with

> his insight into Mississippi, into the consciousness and the mentality of white people who lived in Mississippi and what it was that would be the key to unlocking the situation. . . . He wasn't distracted by school integration. He was for it, but it didn't distract him from the centrality of the right to vote. . . . Somehow, in following his guidance there, we stumbled on the key—the right to vote and the political action that ensued.[11]

MISSISSIPPI FREEDOM RIDERS

In 1960, the bus stations and train stations in Mississippi were all segregated. Blacks were forced into separate waiting rooms, which were usually filthy. In those waiting rooms, they had no access to food or rest rooms. Then in 1961, the Freedom Riders entered Mississippi, and the struggle for equality moved into another dimension. With the cooperation of SNCC, CORE brought students and other outsiders to confront the people in power, to change the laws and end segregation in public transportation facilities. Many of these Freedom Riders were arrested. At first they were placed in the Hinds County jail. Later they were transferred to Parchman State Penitentiary.

Some of the Riders, from the Los Angeles chapter of CORE, were Mary Hamilton, David Richards, Bob and Helen Singleton, and Herbert Mann, who had been in a concentration camp in Germany.

Upon arrival in Parchman, they were stripped of

all of their belongings, even their shoes and combs. The prisoners were each given a striped penitentiary outfit, a bar of soap, a toothbrush, a towel, sheets, and a pillowcase. They were locked up in the maximum-security units reserved for the most hardened criminals. Whites and blacks were segregated in alternate uncleaned cells filled with bugs.

Prisoners could talk back and forth if they did so quietly, but no singing was allowed. If a guard heard singing or thought someone was talking too loudly, everybody's mattress was taken first. Then the sheets, the towels, the soap . . . on down the line, until the prisoners were left with nothing. The Freedom Riders decided to keep singing to maintain their spiritual strength and their unity.

SNCC IN MISSISSIPPI

At the time the Freedom Riders were entering Mississippi, Robert Kennedy, who was then attorney general of the United States, was pressuring those active in the movement to cool things down for a while. The Taconic and Field foundations were willing to grant funds for a voter registration project, and the Justice Department argued that its officials' services could be more effective in dealing with cases that violated voting rights than with sit-in cases. Tim Jenkins, a black student, who was then head of the National Student Association, urged SNCC to take advantage of the foundations' offers and move out of direct action into voter registration exclusively.[12] The leadership of SNCC did not want to forego direct action. Therefore, it decided to have a two-pronged program in Mississippi—direct action *and* voter registration.

To dispense the grants, the Federal Voter Education Project came into being under the auspices of the Southern Regional Council, which was based in Atlanta, Georgia.

Bob Moses returned to Mississippi in July of 1961 as a SNCC staff person to work with Amzie Moore on voter registration. Amzie Moore:

> I knew Bob was a graduate from Harvard and had taught school in New York. I felt like if a man was educated, there wasn't very much you could tell him. I didn't think you could give him any advice. To be honest with you, Bob was altogether different. Bob believed me and was willing to work with me. When I found out he was honestly seeking to help, then in any way I could, I was willing to help him.[13]

Amzie's experience with SNCC turned out to be quite different from his work with the NAACP.

He said:

> I had worked with [Mississippi NAACP leader] Aaron Henry; I did everything I knew how. Every time we moved, we had to move according to law. Unless we were advised to do certain things, we didn't do it. But when SNCC came, it didn't seem to matter what these white people thought. When SNCC moved, SNCC moved in SNCC's way. I'll tell you one thing—the only thing in the twentieth century that gave courage and determination to blacks in the South is SNCC.[14]

Diane Nash, who was now married to James Bevel, another SNCC worker, served as director of the direct-

Bob Moses instructs young volunteers for Freedom Summer, alerting them to the dangers faced in voter-registration campaigns.

Schomberg Center for Research in Black Culture
New York Public Library

action prong of the movement. Along with Bob Moses, Lester McKinney, and Paul Brooks and Katherine Burke, two Freedom Riders, Diane set up a "freedom house" in Jackson. That summer, students from the Freedom Riders—now out of jail—stayed over. Other SNCC workers joined them: James Bevel, Luvaughn Brown, James Dennis, Doris Ladney, and Lawrence Guyot. A rush of activity began all over the Delta.

On August 7, a voter registration school was started in McComb in Pike County; on the fifteenth, three people, an elderly farmer and two middle-aged women who lived in Amite County, went to Liberty to register. Bob tells what happened:

> We left early morning. . . . It was Tuesday. We arrived at the court house about 10 o'clock. The registrar came out. I waited by the side, waiting for either the farmer or one of the two ladies to say something to the registrar. He asked them: What did they want? What were they here for? In a very rough tone of voice. They didn't say anything. They were literally paralyzed with fear. So after a while I spoke up. He asked: Who are you? What do you have to do with them? Do you want to register? I told him who I was and that we were conducting a school in McComb, and these people had attended the school, and they wanted an opportunity to register. Well, he said, they'll have to wait. . . . Our people started to register, one at a time. In the meantime a procession of people began moving in and out of the registration office; the sheriff, a couple of his deputies, people from the far office, the people who do the drivers' licenses— looking in, staring, moving back out, muttering. Finally finished the whole process about 4:30; all three of the people had a chance to register—at least fill out the form. This was a victory.[15]

Just to complete the form was a triumph, for many were not permitted to do that. People qualified to vote were afraid that if they asked for the registration form, they could lose their jobs, but worse than that, they could lose their lives.

BITTER FRUITS OF SMALL VICTORY

Three days later, the first sit-in took place in McComb; Curtis Hayes and Bob Hollis sat in at a Woolworth store, along with sixteen-year-old high-school student Brenda Travis. They were immediately arrested and sentenced to thirty days or a five-thousand-dollar bond. When released, Brenda, a minor, was expelled from school and sent to a juvenile detention camp for six months.

On September 25, Herbert Lee, a farmer, father of ten children, was shot to death for participating in the voter registration project. The killer was Eugene Hurst, a state representative. Four days later more people went to the courthouse to register, and Bob Moses was attacked with the butt of a knife and had to have eight stitches in his head. Bob brought charges of assault and battery against the attacker, Billy Jack Caston. The courtroom was filled with whites who had shotguns. Bob testified, but before the verdict, the sheriff advised him to leave the county. He escorted Bob to the county line. As had been expected, Billy Jack was acquitted by an all-white jury.[16] Bob, of course, stayed on in Mississippi.

Early in October, 115 high-school students demonstrated to protest the murder of Lee and the expulsion of Brenda Travis. All were suspended and notified that if they were not back in school on October 16, they, too, would face expulsion. On the sixteenth, the students returned en masse, deposited their books, and walked out of the school. The Nonviolent High School was opened in Pike County so that they could keep up their studies. Diane Nash Bevel, who taught in the school, was arrested for contributing to the delinquency of minors. She was four months pregnant. After a short time, she was released.

At Diane's trial, two of her students, Jesse Harris and Luvaughn Brown, were arrested when they refused to sit in the "colored" section of the courtroom. They were taken to the county jail. Jesse was beaten and put in the sweatbox on a diet of bread and water. Luvaughn was beaten also. After forty days they were released.

More than three hundred persons were arrested and thousands of dollars in bond money were paid in that year. Many beatings, a murder, and threats of murder brought SNCC face-to-face with the boot and fist of apartheid. SNCC members retreated. Some of their members lived with Amzie in Cleveland. There they organized for the fiercer struggle ahead, a struggle in which SCLC (Southern Christian Leadership Conference) representative Annelle Ponder was so badly beaten she was only able to whisper one word: "Freedom."[17]

If you miss me from the movement and
you can't find me nowhere
Just come on over to the graveyard
I'll be buried there.

—Freedom song

8. *DOWN IN THE DELTA*

When SNCC *workers went to Cleveland, which was deeper*
in the Delta and likely to be far less friendly than Jackson, they knew that their work would not be easy. Why
did they do it? Why risk their lives?

They were young. They knew that what they were
doing was right. Some, especially those born and reared
in the South, had a strong religious faith. They believed
their faith would carry them through any danger. Many
believed that, just maybe, they could influence the Justice Department in Washington to help them secure voting rights for blacks in Mississippi.

Still suffering jailings, beatings, and threats of murder in the Delta, Bob Moses, representing SNCC, and Dave Dennis of CORE met with Medgar Evers and Aaron Henry of the NAACP and reorganized the Council of Federated Organizations (COFO), originally founded in 1955. The main purpose of this restructuring was to combine the efforts of the four major civil rights groups. An executive committee was formed, consisting of Dave Dennis of CORE, Aaron Henry of the NAACP, Bob Moses of SNCC, and Annelle Ponder of SCLC. COFO became the umbrella under which the voter registration drive was to continue. However, SNCC still provided most of the workers who conducted voter education and escorted people to polling places.

The workers went about canvassing from door to door, inviting people to come to churches to learn about getting registered, and to go down to the courthouses to file for registration.

By summer of 1962, SNCC workers had spread out in the Delta, into such places as Greenville, Cleveland, and Ruleville. Curtis Hayes and Hollis Watkins were in Hattiesburg, where they met Victoria Gray, a staunch member of the black community, who later figured prominently in the Mississippi Challenge.

Victoria Gray helped Curtis Hayes and Hollis Watkins organize in Hattiesburg. Each day, in the terrific heat, workers went from door to door asking people to come out to meetings. Often people were afraid to talk to them.

Diane Nash Bevel remembers her work in Sunflower County, in the rural town of Shaw. The popula-

Long lines of demonstrators marched to courthouses to register. Most were unsuccessful.

Courtesy of the L. Zenobia Coleman Library
Tougaloo College

tion of about twelve hundred was half black. The workers tried to reach every black in the town. People would respond, "We heard about the movement. You ain't gon' git these people out. We don't stick together. They ain't coming." SNCC's response was, "If it's just me and you there, will you come?" That night the church overflowed. James Bevel talked about how action makes change.

At one meeting, Fannie Lou Hamer, a sharecropper, became involved in the voter registration project. She, too, later figured prominently in the Challenge. Mrs. Hamer was born in Ruleville, in Sunflower County, the county in which Senator James Eastland, who bitterly opposed voting rights for blacks, lived. Listening to SNCC workers, she saw the possibility of a world she had only imagined.

> "Just listenin' at 'em," she recalled, "I could see myself votin' people out of office I know was wrong and didn't do nothin' to help the poor. I said, you know, that's sumin' I wanna be involved in."[1]

The day after that meeting, August 31, 1962, Mrs. Hamer and seventeen others went into Indianola to register to vote. When she returned, this is what happened at the plantation where she had worked as a timekeeper and sharecropper for eighteen years, and where her husband had worked for forty years:

> That night I was told by a friend that Mr. Marlowe had been telling everybody in the field what he was going to do to me, if I didn't go back and take my name off the book. . . . Marlowe came to the house. . . . I could hear

him telling my husband what he was going to do to me if I did not withdraw. . . . So I went to the door. . . . Marlowe asked me why I went to register. I told him that I did it for myself not for him. He told me to get off the plantation and don't be seen near it again. That night I left . . . and went to stay with Mr. and Mrs. Tucker in Ruleville.[2]

Ten days later a car drove by late at night, and sixteen bullets were fired into the bedroom where Mrs. Hamer slept. She was not at home, and no one was hurt. Mrs. Hamer became a SNCC worker. With her knowledge of the people and her strong sense of fairness and justice, she was a great asset to the movement. Her soul-stirring songs and words of wisdom gave courage to others.

With more and more native Mississippians getting involved, more and more blacks were willing to trust the SNCC workers. They began to believe that SNCC was there to really help them, not to come in, stir things up, and then leave them in the mouth of the wolf.

Early in 1962, Sam Block, a native of Mississippi and a SNCC worker, set up a voter registration project in Greenwood, a town in LeFlore County, the county in which Emmett Till had been murdered seven years earlier. Blacks outnumbered whites in the county, yet only 2 percent of them were registered, compared to 95 percent of whites.

Generally, after the cotton season ended, federal commodities were given to the sharecroppers and their families to tide them over until the start of the cotton season in the spring. That winter, the county officials claimed a lack of funds to distribute the commodities.

Some twenty-two thousand LeFlore County residents, most of them blacks, were without any assistance.

SNCC workers felt responsible for the sharecroppers and started a food drive. SNCC and Friends of SNCC around the country sent in truckloads of food. While they were distributing food, SNCC workers came into contact with thousands of blacks in LeFlore County. More people became involved in the voting project. Hundreds lined up to register. Still, there were many arrests and much harassment. Sam Block was arrested, and hundreds protested.

Bob Moses, in a letter to Friends of SNCC in Chicago thanking them and Dick Gregory, the comedian and activist, reported some other things that happened:

> We have been on a deep plateau all winter, shaking off the effects of the violence of August and September and the eruption that was Meredith at Old Miss [James Meredith had enrolled at the University of Mississippi, September 1962. Two people were killed, 28 federal marshals shot, and 160 injured]. . . . After more than six hundred lined up to receive food in Greenwood on Wednesday, 20 February and Sam's subsequent arrest and weekend in prison on Thursday, 21 February, over one hundred people overflowed city hall to protest at his trial. . . .[3]

The letter revealed how over 250 gathered at a mass meeting that same night, and by 10:30 A.M. on Tuesday, February 26, over 50 people stood in a silent line at the county courthouse; over 200 stood in line that day. "Negroes have never stood en masse in protest at the seat of power in the iceberg of Mississippi politics. . . ." Bob expressed relief at the absence of violence at the

111

courthouse and wondered what would come next because people wanted to vote.

VIOLENCE ESCALATES

At about ten-thirty that evening, Bob found out what was to happen next. He was driving to Greenville from Greenwood with two other workers, one of them James Travis, a Mississippian who had joined SNCC after getting out of jail as a Freedom Rider. An unmarked car pulled alongside them and blasted their car with thirteen .45-caliber bullets. Only Travis was shot, in the shoulder and neck. Luckily, he lived.

This wanton violence enraged many people. One of the most outraged was Wiley Branton, a black native of Mississippi, an attorney who then was director of the Federal Voter Education Project in Atlanta, Georgia. Branton was the great-grandson of Greenwood LeFlore, the former white slave owner for whom the town and the county were named. Seeing the economic reprisals, beatings, and, finally, the violence against Travis, Branton declared:

> The state of Mississippi has repeatedly thrown down a gauntlet at the feet of would-be Negro voters not only by the discriminatory practices of the registrar, but also by the economic pressures, threats, coercions, physical violence and death to Negroes seeking the right to vote. The time has come for us to pick up the gauntlet. Leflore County has selected itself as the testing ground for democracy, and we are accordingly meeting the challenge there.[4]

Branton moved his staff into Mississippi and called

for other civil rights organizations to send workers into Greenwood, too. CORE and SCLC complied. But the violence escalated. A car in front of the SNCC office was riddled with bullets, but none of the three SNCC workers in it were hurt; the SNCC voter registration office was ransacked, phones pulled from the wall, and the place set on fire.

The trouble didn't exist just in Greenwood. There were acts of violence in Jackson and in Clarksdale, where Aaron Henry's drugstore had all the windows broken. Then, on March 26, 1963, shots were fired into the home of Dewey Green, Sr., father of George and Freddie Green, two high-school SNCC workers.[4] Miraculously, no one was hurt.

Lawlessness became more rampant, in spite of the fact that the U.S. Justice Department had finally filed a suit against county and state officials. John Doar, deputy assistant attorney general in the civil rights division, was considered by SNCC workers the most courageous and most accessible government official. Doar said,

> Greenwood was a tough place, a really tough place. . . . We brought suits against the county officials and the state officials and they were in court on these cases of intimidation. At the same time we were trying to get more registrars to open up the rolls. We were battling. We weren't making any significant progress, but we had a lot of presence in Mississippi.[5]

That presence made little difference. The FBI was in Greenwood, but many workers felt that the agents did nothing but take notes as they observed the beatings. Bob Zellner, one of the few white southerners involved in the struggle for voters' rights, received brutal treatment because he was white. Other whites could not understand his behavior and looked upon him as a traitor. After he had been horribly beaten, an enraged man, using his fingers, had tried to dislodge Zellner's eye. Zellner was carried off to jail. Later, an FBI agent told Zellner that agents had witnessed the scene:

> "We didn't want you to think that you were out there by yourself. We were there. We got it all down." [Zellner said he] never had the slightest misapprehension about the FBI from that point on.[6]

The lack of protection, the ever-present danger, and the fear took a toll on everyone. There were constant calls to Washington for help, because the police and law-enforcement agents of the state were part of the problem. No doubt about it, everyone was afraid.

Charles Jones, a SNCC worker who found himself the only one out of jail after a demonstration, was terrified. He felt his life was so endangered that he called Harry Belafonte, the noted singer, actor, and activist. Belafonte located attorney general Robert Kennedy, out in Hollywood at a party. Belafonte gave Jones the number and told him to keep calling Kennedy until he got him. Kennedy told Jones to call John Doar. Charles Jones said,

> I did contact him. And I said to him "Hey we're here. We're down here. We need help." . . . He said, "Okay. I'm coming right in." . . .
>
> Back in the SNCC office that night I heard a knock on the door. I opened the door and John Doar said, whispering: "Hurry, hurry, close the door." Now this is

a representative of the United States of America. He said, whispering again, "Close the door. These people are serious! I'm afraid they're going to kill me. They've been snooping around my motel room. What are we going to do?" . . . At that moment, my disillusionment started. I couldn't imagine this representative of the U.S. government coming in that door, scared, closing it behind him, hiding with me. This was the might of the United States of America, the greatest country in the history of the world, quote-unquote, telling me to close the door and keep the light down and talk quiet.

At that point I knew we were on our own. I mean, that if it was going to happen in the country, we were going to do it. That at best, there would be supports and resources, but this man was scareder than me. In McComb, Mississippi.[7]

The violence continued.

On March 27, 1963, the day after shots were fired into the Greens' house, SNCC called a meeting at a church in Greenwood. The rally turned into a march to the county courthouse, with all the people from the church, about one hundred men, women, and children, singing and praying. They were met by police dogs, along with police wearing yellow helmets and carrying riot sticks. A dog bit one demonstrator and another attacked Bob Moses, tearing his trousers. Bob said:

> We did not anticipate that the police would react as they did. We were simply going to . . . request a conference with the police chief asking for police protection in light of the shooting. They met us with guns and the dogs . . . they simply went berserk for a little while.[8]

Bob Moses, James Forman, the executive director

SNCC workers continued to reach out to African Americans in rural areas.

State Historical Society of Wisconsin

of SNCC, and others were arrested. Moses and Forman were found guilty of disorderly conduct, sentenced to four months in prison, and fined two hundred dollars. The Justice Department intervened and called off its suit against the state officials in return for Moses and Foreman's release.

On June 9 of that year, 1963, Mrs. Hamer, now a SNCC staff member, and five other people, including Annelle Ponder, were on a bus, returning from a meeting in South Carolina. When the bus made a stop in Winona, Mississippi, the police arrested all of them. In the jail they were separated. Soon Mrs. Hamer heard Annelle screaming.

> I knew Annelle's voice. And she was praying for God to forgive them. . . . I was carried to another cell where there was three white men and two Negro prisoners. The state trooper gave one of the Negroes the black jack and he said . . . "I want you to make that bitch wish she was dead. . . ."

The prisoner beat her with the blackjack all over her body, while others held her feet down to keep her from moving. The blackjack was handed to another prisoner, who continued the beating.[9] Mrs. Hamer, who already had a limp from a case of polio as a child, suffered lasting effects from that beating.

Lawrence Guyot, twenty-three-year-old SNCC field secretary, and Milton Hancock drove to Winona to try to see the prisoners. Guyot, a native Mississippian from Pass Christian, was a student at Tougaloo College. State troopers became enraged at Guyot and slapped him

117

several times. They then turned him over to a group of White Citizens Council members. Council members beat him until he couldn't lift his arms and hit him again and again in his face until his eyes were so swollen he couldn't open them. He was then put in jail.

One would think that now the SNCC workers would surely have had enough. Yet, on June 12 they suffered an almost irreparable blow when Medgar Evers was gunned down in the driveway of his home in Jackson. Evers was a quiet, private person, who had proven his fearlessness and love and loyalty to his people as the field secretary of the NAACP. The crushing grief and sorrow of SNCC workers could not last long. They discovered that their most unrelieved tragedy was not death, but the knowledge that anger prevented the natural mourning of their dead. It was this anger, bolstered with love and trust in one another, that kept them moving—knowing that they could make a difference.

The struggle went on.

A DO-IT-YOURSELF ELECTION

Itta Bena is a rural, cotton-growing area just outside Greenwood. Voter registration workers went in to hold a voter-education class there in a small church. Smoke bombs prevented them. When some forty-five people, many of them teenagers, went into Greenwood to protest, they were all arrested. Just a week later, thirteen more young people, some of them from Itta Bena, were also arrested. When they were released, Howard Zinn, the historian and former head of the history department at Spelman College, was there. Zinn says:

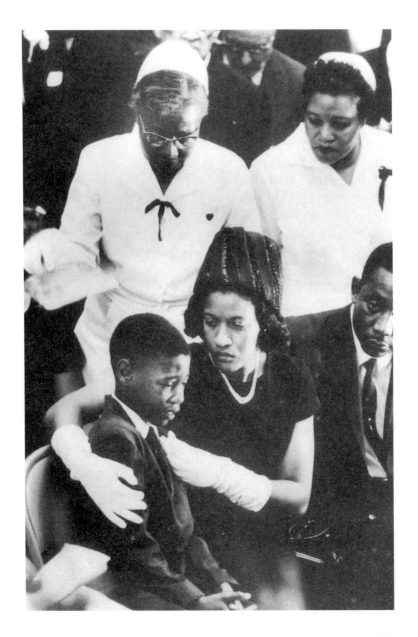

Medgar Evers's widow, seen here at the funeral with one of
their children

New York Public Library

Fifty-eight people were finally freed on bond money supplied by the National Council of Churches. That night SNCC headquarters had the eerie quality of a field hospital after a battle. Youngsters out of jail—sixteen and seventeen years old—were sprawled here and there. Two of them lay on the narrow cots upstairs while a few of the SNCC girls dabbed their eyes with boric acid solution; some dietary deficiency in jail had affected their eyes. One boy nursed an infected hand. Another boy's foot was swollen. He had started to lose feeling in it while in the "hot box" at Parchman penitentiary, and had stamped on it desperately to restore circulation. Medical attention was refused them in prison.[10]

SNCC workers took those young people and a seventy-five-year-old woman, Mother Perkins, who had also spent time in jail, back to Itta Bena. Upon their arrival, there was much joy and spirited singing at a rally. The people in Itta Bena were encouraged to register and let Mississippi officials know that they were there to stay and make their homes safe and free.

By the fall of 1963, so few people had been allowed to register that the possibility of blacks affecting the state and local elections was nil. In November, the Federal Voter Education Project decided to cut funds in Mississippi because more money had been spent there than in any other state, with fewer results. This cut came just before the local and state elections.

Paul Johnson, a Democrat who opposed blacks' enfranchisement, was running for governor against a Republican, Rubel Phillips, equally opposed to blacks. Under the auspices of COFO (the Council of Federated Organizations), a decision was made to hold an election to give all blacks who wanted to vote an opportunity to do so. Bob Moses was named director of the project, Freedom Vote. How could such a project have any effect in a place where those voting in the project had no power?

Mike Thelwell, director of the MFDP (Mississippi Freedom Democratic Party) Washington office during the Challenge, and Lawrence Guyot state that

> while most Negroes could not vote, a Negro could stand for election, and the Negro community could unofficially cast their votes in a parallel election. . . . The entire community could be involved . . . and a people who had been without political exposure for three generations could in this manner be introduced to the mechanics, at least, of political action. . . . These campaigns created a tradition of political involvement in which indigenous leadership could develop. . . .[11]

A large turnout for the Freedom Vote would send a message to those who had for years declared that African Americans were really not interested in voting at all.

Len Holt, a young black southern lawyer active at that time, has suggested another practical reason: The people needed reinforcement, or a reward. Many had to wait months before they knew whether they had passed the voter registration test and become registered voters. Then two or more years might go by before an election. The parallel election served as a reward for those who had put so much on the line to vote.

Aaron Henry ran as candidate for governor and Edwin King, a white minister, chaplain at Tougaloo, an all-black Mississippi college, ran as lieutenant governor.

SNCC staff and mostly white student volunteers from Stanford and Yale spread out across the state, telling people in the cities, the towns, and on the farms and plantations that an election was being held. Interest ran high. Aaron Henry was well known, and Edwin King's credentials as an activist were impressive. He had been arrested four times since 1960 and had been beaten in jail.

The beatings, intimidations, and economic reprisals continued. Nevertheless, the workers placed ballot boxes in churches and meeting places. The candidates spoke to both black and white voters, urging them to end the political and economic dictatorship that had so long run the state.

Unofficial freedom ballots were printed, and six thousand were mailed out to areas where it was too dangerous for SNCC workers to canvass. People in churches, led by the choirs, marched by the ballot box, singing, and cast their ballots. When the campaign was over, some 80,000 blacks had voted—more than three times the total number (23,801) of officially registered black voters in Mississippi.

The organization of the Freedom Vote project across the state was so successful that SNCC workers decided to get more blacks registered. Knowing the danger of their work and how little of that danger was known outside of Mississippi, they also decided to ask more white volunteers to come in. If more whites were involved, the press might take an interest in the project.

Some native Mississippians who had been very active were opposed to bringing a large number of whites into the state. They were concerned about the repercussions of such a move. Whites in an all-black environment would incite violence. Another, more basic reason was put forth by Hollis Watkins, one of the young men who had set up a voter registration project in Hattiesburg in 1961:

> I was against it . . . basically because I felt that we had reached the point where we were making pretty good headway in getting local people from Mississippi involved and getting local people to take the initiative. And I felt that to bring in Northerners would ultimately lead to squashing this initiative. . . . Once it was squashed it would leave those of us . . . who were from Mississippi, who would forever, for the most part, be here, with just that much heavier burden in trying to get people restarted all over again.[12]

Other workers did not feel the same way. Bob Moses, who was highly respected within the group, enthusiastically endorsed the idea, and plans were made to recruit students from solid American families who attended outstanding colleges and universities across the nation. White Americans and the media were far more likely to give attention to the activities of educated, upper-middle-class young whites, and to be far more concerned about their well-being than they were about the safety of young blacks.

Announcement of this plan was made at a big rally and demonstration held in Hattiesburg. Clergymen from all over the nation had been invited to come to Mississippi to participate in a demonstration and show their support for the right of blacks to register and vote.

Under the direction of Lawrence Guyot, the big day was planned for January 22, 1964.

FREEDOM DAY

On January 21, ministers, priests, and rabbis began to arrive in Hattiesburg, a town in southeastern Mississippi. This was the appropriate place for Freedom Day. Mississippi's first sworn affidavit accusing the voter registrar of discrimination had been filed there with the Justice Department in 1949. Plans were under way for a march to city hall for support of a massive voter registration drive. That night, people crowded into a church, filling every seat and aisle, with hardly space for anyone to enter.

The audience was fired up by such speakers as John Lewis from SNCC, who told them the idea of Freedom Summer. There would be freedom schools, art and drama classes, and massive voter registration drives. Annelle Ponder from SCLC and Dave Dennis from CORE also spoke. Aaron Henry, savoring his recent massive victory in the Freedom Vote, was also there. The crowd was pleased to hear from John Pratt, a lawyer from the National Council of Churches. He informed them that the Justice Department had at last (after fifteen years, 1949 to 1963) received the final decision from the Supreme Court to order registrar Theron Lynd to stop requiring blacks to interpret passages from the state constitutions that were different from those used in testing whites. Young Lawrence Guyot was given a rousing welcome. He greeted the crowd and then put forth the plans for Freedom Day.

At the beginning of the meeting, electrical power was shut off, leaving the crowded church in fear and darkness. With a flashlight for speakers, the program continued until the lights came on again. The people were tense, but by the time Guyot finished talking, spirits were high. Someone shouted, "Freedom!" The audience responded, "Now!" Over and over: "Freedom!" "Now!" Everyone then joined hands and sang the song they all had sung many times, "We Shall Overcome."[13] The crowd left, enthusiastic about the next day—Freedom Day.

On Freedom Day it rained. Early that morning, a double line of policemen walked down the streets of Hattiesburg, carrying clubs and clad in yellow rain slickers and red or white or blue helmets. The picket line had already formed at the courthouse: Black and white ministers, with many young black children, were walking in front of the steps. The police marched up and a police car pulled to the curb. From a loudspeaker on the roof of the car, a harsh voice shouted: "This is the Hattiesburg Police Department. We're asking you to disperse. Clear the sidewalk!" No one made a move to leave.

The police, in groups of four, faced the picket line. Still no one moved. Everyone must have thought they all would be arrested. The voice called out: "People who wish to register, line up four at a time and they will be accepted. All those not registering to vote, move off."[14]

The picket line remained undisturbed. It was reinforced by more young black children, some carrying signs asking that their parents be allowed to register.

The scene was peaceful. For the first time in the history of SNCC in Mississippi, blacks and whites were marching together without going to jail. The rain poured at times, but more than a hundred people marched. Still, not more than four people at a time were permitted to enter the courthouse, even though the rain continued most of the day.

Theron Lynd was in charge. Records showed that Lynd had never before registered a single black but had placed 1,836 whites on the rolls without having them fill out the application or interpret sections of the constitution. Until January 30, 1961, not one black had been permitted to fill out a form.[15] The Supreme Court had affirmed a fifth circuit court decision that Lynd was guilty of civil contempt unless he complied with the Court's orders. With news media present, he did his job in a somewhat congenial manner, but he took an hour or more for each four applicants. Those who filled out the forms would have to wait months before they knew whether they had passed the requirements and whether they had been registered as qualified voters.

Freedom Day ended around five o'clock, without mass arrests. There had been only one serious beating that day—Oscar Chase, a student from Yale.[16] And although Bob Moses had been given sixty days in jail and fined two hundred dollars for attempting to make a citizen's arrest of a city official, most of the workers considered Freedom Day a great victory. Some days later, with Bob out of jail, SNCC settled down to make visits to city hall and to plan other activities for Freedom Summer.

When word about the plans for Freedom Summer

Freedom Day rallies, like the one in Hattiesburg, were held
throughout the Deep South. These demonstrators marched
under armed guard in Canton on February 28, 1964.

State Historical Society of Wisconsin

reached Governor Johnson, he called for a special session of the state legislature. They hastily passed bills that would curb further political activity by SNCC. For example, two of these bills outlawed picketing public buildings; freedom schools were prohibited; juveniles arrested for civil rights activities were to be treated as adults; summer volunteers would not be allowed to enter the state.[17]

Bolstered by these strict laws, cities prepared for what the South called "an invasion." Jackson's mayor, Allen Thompson, with a budget of $2 million, increased its police force to twice that of any city of its size. Jackson acquired two horses, six dogs, a tank, and two big detention compounds. "They are not bluffing, we are not bluffing. We're going to be ready for them. . . . They won't have a chance," said Thompson.[18]

In spite of stringent laws and more police enforcement, SNCC and CORE went ahead with their plans and recruited students to work under COFO. SNCC's staff developed a report called "Prospectus for the Summer." Part of that report stated:

> As the winds of change grow stronger, the threatened political elite of Mississippi become more intransigent and fanatical in their support of the status quo. . . . Negro efforts to win the right to vote cannot succeed against the extensive legal weapons and police powers of local and state officials without a nationwide mobilization of support.
>
> Therefore, a program is being planned for this summer which will involve the massive participation of Americans dedicated to the elimination of racial oppression.[19]

I'm sick and tired of being sick and tired.
—Fannie Lou Hamer

9. *A LONG SUMMER FOR FREEDOM*

*T*hat *year, 1964, was a national election year. Both the* Democratic and Republican parties would select their candidates for the presidency of the United States. Early in February, a new idea surfaced. Why not challenge the regular Mississippi delegation to the Democratic National Convention that was to be held that summer in Atlantic City, New Jersey? Such a challenge would call for the support of delegates to the convention from all the other states. Money was needed. The massive task also required a national organizational network. A political party was the ideal vehicle to accomplish that task. Thus was born the Mississippi Freedom Democratic Party (MFDP).

As usual, SNCC had no funds. Appeals went to all the other major civil rights organizations—to become a part of the venture. Only CORE joined. Leaders, such as Bayard Rustin, were not enthusiastic. Creating a third political party in a two-party nation did not strike them as something SNCC could do. However, SNCC, with CORE, pushed on.

On February 23, the California Democratic Council meeting, held in Long Beach, California, endorsed the idea of a challenge.[1] Then at a meeting of liberals (people who were open to political change), Bob Moses met Joseph Rauh. Rauh, an attorney, was then vice president of Americans for Democratic Action (ADA), general counsel for the United Automobile Workers' Union (UAW), and a friend of Senator Hubert Humphrey.[2] At this meeting, Bob spoke about the Challenge.

When Rauh promised his support for the idea, Bob felt that others would join in, and the funds so badly needed would be more easily raised. Ella Baker and Bob Moses went to the UAW convention in Atlantic City to speak to Walter Reuther, president of the UAW. Reuther was not interested.

It was now March, and time was of the essence if the Challenge was to really get off the ground. Again, Rauh was contacted. He agreed to work as legal counsel for the party, without a fee, and gave MFDP the following advice: Participate in the precinct, county, and state conventions of the traditional Mississippi Democrats.

Evidently, he realized immediately that that was almost impossible, so Rauh's second suggestion was: When frustrated, follow procedures approximating as much as possible the procedures of the traditional Democrats. He also advised them to prepare a legal brief to send to the Credentials Committee of the Democratic party, giving reasons why the regular delegation should not be seated.[3]

Time sped by, and the help that was so badly needed did not come. Sensing the urgency, Ella Baker suggested setting up an office in Washington, D.C. By April 24, money had been borrowed and an office opened. Ella Baker coordinated activities with SNCC workers, who earned the regular ten-dollar-a-week salary. Eight workers—Bernard Conn, Barbara Jones, Leslie McLemore, Reginald Robinson, Charles Sherrod, Frank Smith, Alex Stein, and Walt Tillow—wrote letters, made speeches before state delegations, and lobbied Congress for support.[4]

Moses, Guyot, Jesse Morris, and other staffers quickly learned the Democratic party rules in detail. They collected the data that was to be given to the Credentials Committee.

There were still doubts that the plan for a challenge would succeed when the day arrived for the kickoff celebration for MFDP. Meetings had been held across the state to select representatives who would officially organize the party. Precinct captains, precinct workers, voter registration workers, registered voters, and students alike were invited to attend the convention in the Masonic Temple in Jackson on April 26, 1964.

A statewide convention of high-school students who

were interested in voter registration had been scheduled for the twenty-fifth. It drew only eighty-five participants, when hundreds had been expected. Rain may have caused the small turnout. The next day, attendance was equally disappointing. Only two hundred people came. Consistent with SNCC's ability to work with whomever showed, even if it was only one, the MFDP party convened.

Those two hundred people from all over the state of Mississippi elected Lawrence Guyot, chairman of the party; Fannie Lou Hamer, vice chairwoman; Victoria Gray, national committeewoman; Edwin King, national committeeman; and Peggy Jean Connor, secretary.

Counsel Rauh had suggested that MFDP duplicate the things the regular Democrats did. MFDP decided to enter candidates in the primary elections. Workers spread out over the state seeking enough signatures to place four candidates from MFDP on the regular Democratic primary ballot.

The four candidates got on the ballots in time for the June 2 primary election. Mrs. Hamer ran for Congress in the Second Congressional District; Reverend John Cameron ran in the Fifth Congressional District; James Monroe Houston from Vicksburg in the Third Congressional District; and Victoria Gray ran against incumbent Senator John Stennis. Mrs. Hamer echoed the sentiments of the party when she told voters that she was for all the citizens of Mississippi, black and white, having a better life.

Without much time for campaigning, and with the denials of voter registration, intimidation of voters, and the harassment of candidates, none of the four won.

However, documentation was made of this activity. Thousands of names were added to the ninety-three thousand names already on the Freedom Party lists (collected by SNCC throughout the state). The denials, harassment, and intimidations were documented, too, and sent to Atlanta, Georgia, where copies were made on microfilm to use in the legal brief.

PREPARATION FOR
THE NATIONAL CONVENTION

Every state chooses delegates to the national conventions differently. For the Democratic National Convention every precinct in Mississippi is mandated to hold precinct meetings to elect delegates to the county conventions. There are 1,884 voting precincts. Voters at the precinct meetings send delegates to the eighty-two county conventions, which then select delegates from the five congressional districts. Congressional-district delegates select the delegates to the national convention.

In 1964, precinct meetings to begin the process of electing sixty-eight delegates were set for the morning of June 16. Pursuing Rauh's suggestion to follow procedures of the regular Democrats, MFDP tried to attend these precinct meetings. Many members had difficulty finding the designated locations. Many meetings simply were not held. Where they were held, blacks were refused admittance. On that morning, this is what happened in Ruleville:

> Eight negro voters went to the place where the precinct meeting should have been held, the regular polling place. They tried the door . . . it was locked. They called

out, no one answered. Then at 10:05 the negro voters convened the precinct meeting on the lawn of the community house, a resolution was passed pledging support of the National Democratic Party. Delegates were elected for the county convention. After a short prayer and singing "We Shall Overcome," the precinct meeting adjourned. The entire operation was filmed by CBS news, TV.[5]

This type of activity was documented throughout the state by SNCC workers and volunteers. The documentation was sent to the Credentials Committee, as had been suggested by SNCC counsel Rauh. It would help determine who were the legal representatives of the people of Mississippi to the National Democratic Convention, and to prove that Mississippi was in violation of Section 2 of the Fourteenth Amendment of the Constitution. Section 2 prohibits denial of the right to vote in any election of the choice of electors of president and vice president of the United States.

ANOTHER CIVIL RIGHTS ACT

On July 2, 1964, Congress passed the Civil Rights Act, which President Johnson signed. This act had been conceived by President Kennedy in 1963 after four children in Birmingham, Alabama, had been killed by a bomb placed in their Sunday school. The act made it unlawful to discriminate in public places, in hiring, and in voting. It created the Community Relations Service to settle desegregation problems, and it also created the Equal Employment Opportunity Commission (EEOC). In addition, the act extended the Commission on Civil

Rights. This bold approach to ending discrimination gave heart to MFDP. But SNCC and MFDP did not try to integrate public places. Now they were using all of their resources to gain the right to vote, which they saw as the way to gain all other rights.

FREEDOM SUMMER

The summer of 1964 began with bustling, well-publicized activity. The goals had been greeted with contagious enthusiasm in many parts of the nation. The idea of setting up freedom schools in the most educationally deprived area of the nation attracted educators, who prepared an innovative curriculum. Volunteer health professionals from the Medical Committee for Human Rights set up clinics to provide basic health services, unknown in the Delta. Artists and actors came to expand the work of Gil Moses (no relation to Bob) and John O'Neal in the Free Southern Theater. This theater was well known throughout the South for using drama to motivate people to become politically active.

The greatest number of volunteers were students—more than eight hundred—who came from some of the most outstanding colleges and universities in the nation. Many of them were young, requiring the permission of their parents to participate. Because they had to support themselves in Mississippi and provide their own transportation, most of them came from well-to-do families. Less than 10 percent were African Americans.[6]

The volunteers were divided into two major groups: voter registration workers and teachers. These young people bore the brunt of the work in the field, getting people registered and working in the freedom schools. The volunteers had to be trained for nonviolent behavior and made acquainted with the way of life of the people in Mississippi. Some of the volunteers had worked in the civil rights movement in other parts of the South. Most of them had to understand that Mississippi was unlike any place they had visited. The majority of these young men and women had led protected lives in basically all-white environments where poverty and violence were virtually unknown.

Two training sessions of one week each were set up for the volunteers at the Western College for Women in Oxford, Ohio. They were told that living in Mississippi as a SNCC worker meant living on the edge, always alert, watching over one's shoulder, expecting to be arrested, beaten, or, worse, killed. John Doar told them that the federal government would not protect them in Mississippi. Their protection was dependent upon the law-enforcement agencies of the state.[7]

The people who did most of the training were those who had already lived through three years of this risk taking, and the volunteers were awed by them. One volunteer said:

> I've never known people like them before: They are so full of heart and life. They are not afraid to show their emotions; they cry when they are sad; they laugh and dance when they are happy. And they sing; they sing from their hearts and in their songs they tell of life, struggle, sadness and beauty. They have a freeness of spirit that I've rarely seen. But I think that's because they don't worry about the status quo. . . .[8]

Another volunteer foresaw what might happen, when she took a look at fellow workers:

> There is a quiet Negro fellow on the staff who has an ugly scar on his neck and another on his shoulder where he stopped .45 [-caliber] slugs. . . . Another fellow told this morning how his father and later his brother had been shot to death. . . . I'd venture to say that every member of the Mississippi staff has been beaten at least once and he who has not been shot at is rare.[9]

CHANEY, GOODMAN, AND SCHWERNER

James Chaney and Michael Schwerner were at the training session. Schwerner was a twenty-four-year-old white social worker from New York. Chaney was a twenty-one-year-old black native of Meridian, Mississippi. Both men were on the CORE staff, and they had worked together in Meridian to create and run a library for African Americans. They had also participated in voter registration. Schwerner had been in Mississippi for six months and had riled Klan members, who referred to him as Goatee because of the shape of his beard.[10]

At the orientation, Schwerner and Chaney met Andrew Goodman, twenty-one, who was a white student from New York. On Goodman's very first day in Mississippi, June 21, the three young men drove into Neshoba County to look into the burning of Mount Zion Methodist Church. They had planned to use this church for their freedom school. In Philadelphia, the county seat, they were arrested on charges of speeding by Cecil Price, the county deputy sheriff. Late that night, Price released them. Not long after their release, they were stopped by

Price and members of the Ku Klux Klan. When they did not return to Meridian, fear of their having been murdered caused an angry stir. A well-organized search was begun throughout Mississippi.

J. EDGAR HOOVER COMES TO MISSISSIPPI

When word spread that the three civil rights workers were missing, the FBI began its routine of note taking, but the country was in no mood to wait and let the trail of the murderers cool. Under much pressure, President Lyndon Johnson dispatched FBI chief J. Edgar Hoover himself to Jackson, Mississippi, to set up an office for agents to handle the case. Soon hundreds of agents were in Mississippi, aided by searchers from a naval installation at Meridian.

The change of attitude toward murder in Mississippi was remarkably amazing. The rivers and swamps in and around Neshoba County were dredged. Bodies of black men were found, and the press took great interest, until it was discovered that those were not the bodies of the three civil rights workers. Two of these men were former SNCC workers, Charles Moore and Henry Dee. Their deaths were not deemed worthy even of a mention in the news.

While the search continued, the work went on, and the volunteers spread out into the Delta to do the job they had come to do. They were awed by the people, the place, and the poverty.

BREAKING BREAD TOGETHER

These young volunteers, including some who had traveled abroad, settled in with families who knew little about the world beyond the small rural towns where they lived:

> We were immediately invited to live and eat in Negro homes and to speak in Negro churches. For many local citizens, our coming was a religious event. I found it difficult to be cynical. Sometimes when we pass by, the children cheer.[11]

The whites who lived in the homes of black people probably did not realize the effect they were having on the Mississippi culture and basic racial attitudes, but black Mississippians felt the impact of what had once been a closed society being opened up. In many cultures, to break bread is to break barriers. Therefore, when strangers appear, food is shared: bread and salt in the former Soviet Union, the kola nut in some African countries. Over food, a friendly atmosphere is easily established. The ruling-class Mississippians understood this. For blacks and whites to eat together was taboo in the state. That taboo was broken in Unita Blackwell's house:

> I remember cooking some pinto beans—and everybody just got around the pot, you know, and that was an experience just to see white people coming around the pot and getting a bowl, and putting some stuff in and then sitting around talking.[12]

The work was hard, the weather almost unbearably hot, and many blacks were on the road, having been evicted from the plantations and fired from their jobs. Food was scarce, living quarters in many instances uncomfortable, and the psychological stress of fear played havoc on the minds and bodies of SNCC workers. Given the variety of backgrounds and experiences, and the nature of human beings, there were problems.

Some of the black SNCC workers became cynical because some of the volunteers assumed an air of know-all and felt that it was their role to lead. One black volunteer remembers,

> white counterparts as generally a good bunch, but there were . . . a few who just came in and wanted to take over. Their attitude was okay, we are here, your troubles are over. We are going to put your house in order.[13]

One white volunteer admitted his insensitivity toward a black SNCC leader:

> I was always after him about being immoral, irresponsible. . . . I just moved in and took over.[14]

Indeed, at the very beginning, the media did make it appear that the young white students had been recruited not merely to participate in the movement, but to save it.

The problems, many though there were, did not keep these students from working together and overcoming their natural differences. Their accomplishments are now part of the history of this country. And just what did they accomplish? They challenged the belief held in the South, and especially in Mississippi, even after the Civil War, that people of different backgrounds and races can live together only when one is master and the other slave.

Each day during July and August, volunteers went

from door to door throughout the state, urging partici-
pation and taking people to the courthouses to register
to vote. They asked both black and white people to sign
up for the new Mississippi Freedom Democratic Party
(MFDP). For the very first time in the history of Mississippi, a black person, along with a white, sat in the homes
of whites and talked about the political system.

At one home, the team was told by the man of the
house, "I've been a member of the Ku Klux Klan for
years. What do you have to say about that?" Even with
this acknowledgment, there was some feeling that
the man and wife were interested in carrying on the
discussion. The SNCC volunteers continued their
approach and refused to argue. The team left within
a few minutes, without having changed the couple's
minds.

"You people are a bunch of damned fools. You
don't understand Mississippi," the avowed Klansman
declared as the team walked out. However, when they
had walked through the gate, he called them back. He
gave the young woman volunteer a bouquet of red and
yellow roses picked from his garden and said, "Good
luck. But I still think you're crazy."[15]

FREEDOM SCHOOLS

When the idea of Freedom Summer was put forth,
Charley Cobb, a SNCC field secretary, suggested creating an actual summer school for children. The freedom
schools would help blacks learn to question. In his *Notes
on Teaching in Mississippi*, Cobb stated why that goal was
important for black Mississippians:

141

Repression is the law; oppression the way of life. . . . They have learned the lesson necessary for immediate survival: that silence is safest, so volunteer nothing; that the teacher is the state, and tell them only what they want to hear; that the law and learning are white man's law and learning. . . . There is the waiting, not to be taught, but to reach out and meet and join together, and to change. The tiredness of being told it must be, " 'cause that white folks' business," must be met with the insistence that it is their business.[16]

Staughton Lynd, a history professor who had spent time in a cooperative in Georgia and as a teacher at Spelman College, coordinated the Mississippi freedom schools with the help of Elizabeth Fusco and Tom Wahman. The activities were divided into three general areas: academic work, recreation and cultural activities, and leadership development—all to be integrated into one learning experience.

The staff planned for an enrollment of about one thousand students in the tenth, eleventh, and twelfth grades. On July 7, 1964, the freedom schools opened. By the end of summer, three thousand students had been enrolled in grades as low as the fifth, and the twenty schools they had planned for had increased to fifty.[17]

FREEDOM SCHOOL STUDENTS AND TEACHERS

The guiding principle in the freedom schools, for both students and teachers, was flexibility. The main goal was to prepare people for leadership roles. Flexibility permitted not only much younger students to enter the classroom, but older men and women, too, who were anxious for knowledge and eager to explore new ideas.

What did the students learn? How were they affected by Freedom Summer? For the first time in a classroom setting, many of these children were exposed to algebra, to poetry, to role playing, and, most of all, to freedom of creative expression. Many were accustomed to having regular school in churches, lodges, and places other than those designed by the state for formal learning. Therefore, many of them must have expected the regular kind of sessions. How surprised they must have been to have a different kind of challenge.

Students wrote poetry, created newspapers, and talked about their work and their ideas. Such black poets as Langston Hughes were used to motivate them. Ida Ruth Griffin, age thirteen, wrote a poem that stirred controversy among her classmates:

> I am Mississippi-fed
> I am Mississippi-bred
> Nothing but a poor, black boy.
>
> I am a Mississippi slave
> I shall be buried in a Mississippi grave
> Nothing but a poor dead boy.[18]

After she read it, angry silence filled the room. The students, like most young African Americans, found it difficult to identify with their blackness and their political poverty. The first line of defense is denial. And many must have been thinking, "I'm no black slave!" Finally the silence was broken when one brave girl dared speak.

"She's right. We certainly are. Can your papa vote? Can mine? Can our people eat anywhere they want to?"

The teacher, who had listened and watched and waited, was rewarded when lively discussion that proved the students were thinking broke out, replacing the deadly silence and denial.

There is no way to define a *typical* teacher in the freedom schools. However, Dr. Robert Coles, noted child psychiatrist, has detailed the life of one volunteer, Larry.

Larry came to Mississippi from New England. Like other teachers, he lived in the homes of the parents of the students he taught. It was not easy for him. "I try to get them to call me by my first name, but either they won't or they get around it by not using my name at all."[19] Larry did not understand that most black people would not call *any* teacher by his or her first name. The barrier was twofold: race and class. He didn't especially like the food, and the grammar of the children appalled him. But after trying to change the students to his way of thinking and talking, he decided that maybe the problem was as much his as theirs. Dr. Coles tells of Larry's solution:

> Perhaps he should let that be rather than fight it. He should try to teach the children pride in their race's history ... its writers, singers and artists; its men of science and learning. "I didn't know about those people myself until I got involved in this project. All I knew was that the Negro had been almost destroyed by slavery and persecution. It never occurred to me that he had really built a very significant culture of his own."[20]

Larry relaxed with the black families and the students and was able to teach. But the fear of the whites lingered. All of the volunteers were aware that the search for Chaney, Goodman, and Schwerner was still going on, and that the churches and houses of people involved in the freedom schools were being bombed. Shopping for razor blades or picking up his mail at the post office was painful for Larry. The inability to worship in a white church, the glares, stares, and hostile words from white people bothered him. At night he was afraid of dynamite. The deep fission in the black and white world became real to him.

In spite of all the fear, Larry was able to remain in Mississippi that summer. Then, like many of the teachers, he left to return to his studies. It is quite possible that many of them felt the way he did as he was leaving:

> I kept wondering how I could face it; the silliness and emptiness; the instructors who think they're god because they've read a few books and can sit and talk about "ideas"; the ivy that doesn't only climb the buildings but grows up the legs and into the brains of both teachers and students. What would a football game mean to me? A spring riot over nothing? A rule about wearing a tie at breakfast? I could hear all those instructors telling me how "complicated" everything is, and how "practical" you have to be, and how more "research" has to be done; and I knew I would do one of three things: cry to myself, scream at them, or just smile.[21]

SOME SIGNIFICANT OTHERS

Early in the SNCC movement in Hattiesburg, the National Council of Churches had maintained support.

It provided funds for child-care centers and assisted MFDP in teaching citizenship classes and in other ways aided the struggle. Now, in the months between May and September, 400 ministers, priests, and rabbis worked in Mississippi under the sponsorship of the National Council of Churches. These clergymen gave spiritual guidance and also performed religious services for the volunteers when many local churches refused to do so.

About 150 lawyers were in the state to give legal advice and to help Freedom Summer volunteers avoid longer jail terms and higher bail bonds. There also were about 100 doctors and health professionals, including nurses and psychologists. They were badly needed to take care of the illnesses and injuries and to help heal the minds that were damaged by trauma and fear.

Many of these people left Mississippi more dedicated than when they had come. Some admitted that they had not witnessed such cold, brutal treatment of human beings ever before. The clergymen were treated no differently from all the others. They, too, were beaten, some unmercifully.[22]

CIVIL RIGHTS WORKERS FOUND

Still under pressure from President Johnson, the FBI decided that someone would talk if they made it worthwhile, so they began to spend thousands of dollars for information. That effort paid off, and the bodies of Chaney, Goodman, and Schwerner were discovered on August 4, underneath a dam.[23]

An expert pathologist, Dr. David Spain, called in to conduct an independent examination of James Chaney's body, recalled,

146

I could barely believe the destruction to these fragile young bones. In my twenty-five years as a pathologist and medical examiner, I have never seen bones so severely shattered, except in tremendously high-speed accidents or airplane crashes. . . . It was difficult to retain my professional composure. . . . I felt like screaming at those impassive observers still silently standing across the table.[24]

SNCC workers believed that those guilty of the murders were likely to go unpunished unless federal agencies intervened, but the government does not call murder a federal offense in the United States. Therefore, civil rights activists urged the Justice Department to charge the murderers with denying the civil rights of Chaney, Goodman, and Schwerner. Nineteen men were formally charged. For the first time in the movement, pressure was applied, and the FBI began to do more than just witness events, "writing it all down." Still, the beatings and the damaging fear remained rampant.

When Freedom Summer ended, there were criticisms of the program. Widespread stories claimed that SNCC's staff people were incapable of creating such an idea and executing such a program. Their success was attributed to the Communist party. It is to the credit of SNCC workers that they did not succumb to these pressures and begin screening people for their political beliefs rather than for their abilities to adhere to the principles of nonviolence and to work with others regardless of race, creed, and color.

By August of 1964, SNCC had accomplished a perilous and herculean task. About seventeen thousand blacks attempted to register to vote. Some sixteen hundred were actually registered. Thousands signed up for the Mississippi Freedom Democratic Party, and some of the freedom schools were extended. It was SNCC's first attempt to put alternative learning institutions in place.[25]

The success of Freedom Summer was marred by fear and danger. Fred Powledge says:

> The terror was widespread. . . . There were six murders . . . thirty shootings, in which three persons were injured; thirty homes and businesses were bombed; thirty-five churches were bombed or burned; and there were at least eighty beatings.[26]

The job was not finished. More time would now be spent in expanding the MFDP. The idea of challenging Mississippi's racist voting practices remained very much alive. That project was next in line.

10. *ATLANTIC CITY BOUND*

August 6, just two days after the bodies of Chaney, Goodman, and Schwerner had been found, the state convention for MFDP was held in Jackson to choose sixty-eight delegates to the Democratic National Convention. Hundreds of voter registration workers from all over the state attended. Ella Baker, the keynote speaker, expressing the outrage of the community at the murders, gave a stirring address. She let everyone know that this was the moment for black people to demand the end to acceptance of the illegal government of Mississippi and the people elected under its illegal laws.

149

One of the Freedom Summer volunteers had the opportunity to attend the MFDP convention. She described her feelings there:

> This is the most exciting, moving and impressive thing I have ever had the pleasure of witnessing—let alone be a part of.
>
> Miss Ella Baker presented a very stirring keynote address. . . . Right after Miss Baker's speech, there was a march of all the delegates around the convention hall— singing Freedom Songs, waving American flags, banners and county signs. This was probably the most soul-felt march ever to occur in a political convention, I felt, as we marched with a mixture of sadness and joy—of humility and pride—of fear and courage, singing "Go Tell It on the Mountain," "Ain't Gonna Let Nobody Turn Me Round," and "This Little Light of Mine." You would just . . . have to be here to really feel . . . what it means to the people who are here.[1]

Chairman Lawrence Guyot received instructions from the members of MFDP to send a letter to John Bailey, the national committee chairman of the Democratic party, calling for the seating of the MFDP delegation at the party's national convention under the Fourteenth Amendment.

With this feeling of faith in the American institutions and in the American people, the sixty-eight delegates and alternates, four of them white, set out for Atlantic City. The group included ordinary citizens, sharecroppers, day laborers, beauticians, barbers, and preachers. Some had never been out of their counties. What would happen when they got there? How would they be received? They were filled with awe at what they had achieved. They were exhilarated at being on their

MFDP delegates prepare to board the bus to the Democratic
National Convention in Atlantic City.

Courtesy of the L. Zenobia Coleman Library
Tougaloo College

way to participate in national politics. They were going to show the nation that they were there to represent not only the black people of Mississippi but *all* oppressed people.

CHALLENGE NUMBER ONE

MFDP members had a chance of unseating the regular Mississippi delegates, but there were some problems.

The Republicans had chosen Barry Goldwater of Phoenix, Arizona, as their candidate just a few days after President Johnson signed the Civil Rights Act. Goldwater promoted a plan to woo southern Democrats by placing emphasis on racial discord and the fear of whites that blacks were moving too fast toward equality. He believed he could win the presidency with southern and conservative votes, without blacks and liberals.

George Wallace, governor of Alabama, had campaigned on a racist platform in the Democratic primaries and had done well in Maryland, Wisconsin, and Indiana. The race question polarized the nation, and fear made both major parties more conservative.

The regular Mississippi delegation knew that President Johnson did not want to alienate the South. They also went to Atlantic City aware of the June 30 Mississippi state Democratic party platform, which was against civil rights, poll-tax amendments, and the United Nations. The state party also rejected the platforms and candidates of both the Republican and Democratic parties, and the majority, sixty-five of sixty-eight, refused to declare their loyalty and support to the persons cho-

sen to run on the Democratic ticket. Mississippi delegates to the national convention were not bound by the
voters to support the party candidates. What candidates
Mississippians would support would be determined at
the state convention held *after* the national convention.

On August 13, the Jackson *Daily News* reported that
Governor Paul B. Johnson received a call from President
Lyndon Baines Johnson assuring him of two things:

1. The three loyal delegates of the regular
   Mississippi delegation would be seated as the
   other sixty-five stalked out in indignation at
   being asked to take an oath of loyalty to the
   party.
2. The [Mississippi] Freedom Democratic Party
   would not be allowed as part of the Mississippi
   delegation.[2]

President Johnson knew that even though most of the
Mississippi regulars would walk out of the convention,
some had to stay to keep MFDP from being seated by
default.

Len Holt has described such plans as a "script to be
followed at Johnson's Convention." As part of the script,
Johnson decided not to name a running mate before
the convention. The two main choices for vice president
were Senator Hubert Humphrey, the choice of the powerful UAW (United Auto Workers) and the ADA
(Americans for Democratic Action) and other liberals;
and David Lawrence, head of the Credentials Committee. Lawrence, in charge of that committee, had much
influence on which delegation was seated. Johnson

thought that their competition for the vice presidency would bring some drama to the convention.

Governor Carl Sanders of Georgia was made head of the Rules Committee, to serve the purposes of the Great Society. The script called for the unseated MFDP to enter the halls triumphantly as "honored guests"— anything except as the Mississippi delegation.[3]

When MFDP arrived in Atlantic City during the week of August 22, it had some advantages, too. First, it had overwhelming evidence that the regulars were illegally chosen to represent the people of Mississippi. The recent murders of the three young civil rights workers, Chaney, Goodman, and Schwerner, were fresh in the minds of most Americans. MFDP also had the support of as many as nine delegations, including those of major states such as Michigan, California, Oregon, and New York. Such members of Congress as William Fitts Ryan of New York; Edith Green of Oregon; Gus Hawkins, Phil Burton, and James Roosevelt of California; and Robert Kastenmeier of Wisconsin supported the MFDP delegation's right to be seated.[4]

MFDP members were determined to be recognized as the true representatives of the people of Mississippi. They had not come through blood, sweat, and tears just to be seen and heard. They had come to take their seats in the convention hall and vote on national issues. They knew that peril to their lives still existed. On August 13, the attorney general of Mississippi had issued an injunction against MFDP in the state's courts. The threat of being jailed for going to the convention hung over their heads.[5] But the delegates knew how they had gotten there and why they were there and what they had come for. They were set on getting it in the end. Victoria Gray expressed their determination well:

> We came with nothing, and we realized that it made no sense at all, with all the risk that had been, to accept what we knew for certain to be nothing and to go back there to God only knows what. You may get home and not have a house. You may get home and a member of your family might be missing. You may not get home at all, and so you know we are not going to accept anything less than what we came after, which is the real thing—representation and the right to participate. And if we don't get that, then we'll go back and take our chances and regroup and come to fight another day. . . .[6]

On August 22, MFDP presented its credentials, and the news media focused U.S. attention on the group. Here were these "grassroots people," trying to upset the power of Mississippi. For more than seventy-five years, Mississippi had been permitted to perform its and the nation's business without a constitution ratified by its citizens. Who were these people who assumed that they could do the impossible?

Fannie Lou Hamer was now known as "the former sharecropper" from the town of Ruleville, in Sunflower County. She described, with clarity and great emotion, how she had been jailed. She left out nothing. The nation watched as she told how her dress had been raised and how she had been beaten with a blackjack by black prisoners while white sheriffs urged them on. The world saw this drama, and President Johnson hastily called a news conference to draw attention away from Mrs.

Hamer and the parents of Chaney, Goodman, and Schwerner, who had come to lend support to the Challenge. But enough had been seen and heard. More delegates began to consider giving support to MFDP. For three days the Credentials Committee was deadlocked on the issue. The wheels of the system began to turn. The president made it known that if the UAW and ADA wanted Senator Humphrey as his running mate for vice president, then they must use their forces to get MFDP to accept what he called an "at-large" status.

At large usually means that delegates may be seated but may not represent the districts from which they were elected; they may represent the area, city or state, as a whole. Further, they may have no votes. In reality MFDP members were being offered "guest of the convention" status. They would represent *no place at all* and would not vote. Walter Reuther, who was in negotiations for a labor contract, was summoned to Atlantic City to bring Joseph Rauh, his general counsel, who had advised MFDP, in line with the proposition.

Rauh was asked to talk to MFDP delegates and get them to accept the at-large status. The delegation refused. To reinforce the president's wishes, black leaders, such as Roy Wilkins, head of the NAACP; James Farmer of CORE; Martin Luther King, Jr., of SCLC (Southern Christian Leadership Conference); Congressman Charles Diggs of Michigan; and Congressman William Dawson of Chicago, were summoned by Humphrey's forces to meet with MFDP. They pressured MFDP to accept the offer and keep unity in the Democratic party so that Goldwater would not win the presidency. Dr.

King, who had gone to the convention supporting the group, now urged it to compromise. MFDP held out. The delegates could not accept a position that left them out of all the proceedings.

MFDP knew that more members of the Credentials Committee had been moved by their testimony. A roll call of the convention might reveal others who were on its side. It needed eleven people on the Credentials Committee to sign a minority report calling for the seating of MFDP. The Freedom Democrats knew they had nine supporters, including Rauh and Congressman Diggs. They needed eight delegations to ask for a roll call. Counting on the District of Columbia, Guam, Puerto Rico, and the Virgin Islands, they felt sure of success.[7] But when it was learned that these territories were involved, Governor Sanders made a change in rules: Only states—not territories—could request a roll call. That took care of the eight needed delegations.

Other tactics were used. Congressman Diggs pressured Bob Moses for the names of members of the Credentials Committee who supported signing the minority report calling for the seating of MFDP. Moses was reluctant to share that information. Diggs said he wanted "to give the names to David Lawrence [Credentials Committee chairman] to show him we [MFDP] have the strength to pull a minority vote on the floor." Instead, the list was used to intimidate those who were willing to sign the minority report.[8]

James Forman said, "We do not know all the forms of the great squeeze, but we do know that a telephone call was made to one delegate from California by someone saying that her husband would not get his appointment as a federal judge if she voted for the minority position. She backed out, sorrowfully. . . ."[9] In the end, both Rauh and Congressman Diggs refused to sign the minority report. The support for the minority report dropped from eighteen to only four members of the Credentials Committee.[10]

Without consulting MFDP, a further compromise offer was made to give at-large delegate status to two persons selected by Hubert Humphrey: Aaron Henry and Rev. Edwin King.[11] They would be given a token vote. On Tuesday, August 25, the Credentials Committee decided upon this recommendation:

> Wholly apart from the question of the contest as to the delegates from Mississippi and in recognition of the unusual circumstances presented at the hearing and without setting any precedent for the future, it is recommended that Dr. Aaron Henry, chairman, and the Reverend Edwin King, national committeeman-designate, of the Freedom Democratic Party, be accorded full delegate status, in a special category of the delegates-at-large of this convention, to be seated as the chairman of the convention may direct.[12]

MFDP delegates were angry about the kind of tactics that were being used. "It's a token of rights on the back row that we get in Mississippi. We didn't come all this way for that mess again," said Mrs. Hamer. They had come with faith in the system's fairness. They began to doubt what they had believed: that if the nation only knew what was happening in Mississippi, justice would prevail.

Turmoil still existed. Something had to be done to keep MFDP from destroying the president's plan to keep the southerners in his camp. Aaron Henry, chairman of the delegation, wanted to accept the offer that was made to seat him and Edwin King, one of the four whites in the delegation. The others were very angry and considered the fact that Senator Humphrey had chosen those two delegates an insult. At least they should have been able to choose their own representatives. Mrs. Hamer certainly would have been elected. They refused to accept the offer.

They would accept instead the compromise that Congresswoman Edith Green of Oregon had proposed. Congresswoman Green offered to administer a Democratic party loyalty oath to both MFDP and the regular Mississippi delegates, and to say that those who took the oath had become the representatives, with the votes being equally divided between the regulars and MFDP. Seven people on the Credentials Committee voted with her, but twelve votes were needed.

That night (August 25) at the opening session, MFDP, showing that it wanted nothing less than true representation, sat in the seats designated for the Mississippi delegation. There was a terrific stir. Sergeants at arms were ready to use force to get them out, but knowing how sit-ins worked, they knew they would have had to drag MFDP out bodily. That would have been too much for the world to see. A call came, possibly from the president himself, saying that the delegation should remain seated. The MFDP heard the doubtful voice vote of the convention adopt the final recommendation of the Credentials Committee:

> We recommend that the members of the delegation of the Freedom Democratic Party . . . be welcomed as honored guests of this convention . . . that Dr. Aaron Henry, chairman, and the Reverend Edwin King, national committeeman-designate of the Freedom Democratic Party, be accorded full delegate status in a special category of delegates-at-large of this convention, to be seated as the chairman of the convention may direct.[13]

The next morning, August 26, the MFDP delegates met at the Union Temple Baptist Church. They now knew that Aaron Henry, Edwin King, and Dr. Martin Luther King, Jr., had agreed to the at-large plan and to Senator Humphrey's naming of the two delegates.[14]

Aaron Henry persuaded them to hear the arguments of black leaders and of others in the Democratic party. On the afternoon of the twenty-sixth, President Johnson's "best and brightest" put forth their arguments. Senator Wayne Morris declared that MFDP had won a "victory" that should be accepted. Dr. Martin Luther King, Jr., tried to convince them with his well-known eloquence: "This is the greatest decision you'll ever have to make in your lifetime. And the weight of this decision will affect not only what takes place in America, but throughout the world." He brought promises from Hubert Humphrey that things would change in Mississippi after the election and that a meeting with President Johnson was assured.[15]

They were told to accept the decision so that MFDP could participate in a grand ceremony, a march into the convention, with the eyes of the world upon them. The chairman would call out to the two delegates-at-large; then Aaron Henry would get a chance to say, "I, Aaron Henry . . . cast two votes for President Lyndon B. Johnson."[16] MFDP was advised to accept and maintain the good relations it had with Walter Reuther and labor. The delegates listened and then went into a closed-door session alone.

They emerged still believing that they had come to represent all those black people in Mississippi who had faced joblessness, starvation, even death so that they could come to Atlantic City to cast their votes. They had not come merely to be seen or to be heard. They had come to participate. They had come to vote, to share in the hammering out of issues, and to have a voice in naming the standard-bearer of the Democratic party. Being seated to represent Mississippi was their right. It was their responsibility to replace those who were illegally chosen and were being illegally accepted by that convention. Their answer was still *no!*

When President Johnson got word of their answer, he decided to break a precedent and come onto the convention floor before he had been nominated. The spotlight must not be on those sharecroppers and farmers and grassroots people.

When the Mississippi Freedom Democrats arrived at the convention hall, all but three of the seats designated for the Mississippi delegation had been dismantled. What appeared to be FBI agents or armed security guards surrounded the three white regular delegates, while the sixty-eight members of the MFDP delegation stood where they felt they should have been seated.

Those Mississippi blacks back home and other blacks across the nation who witnessed the scene will probably always remember that proud moment.

MFDP delegates left Atlantic City with many in the nation feeling that they had been defeated. Of course, they had not achieved what they had come for, and some of them were angry, some disillusioned. They had learned a bitter lesson, expressed by James Forman:

> No longer was there any hope, among those who still had it, that the federal government would change the situation in the deep south. The fine line . . . between the state governments and the federal government which we had used to build a movement had played out.[17]

The independence of MFDP angered some of the liberals, who felt that protest and politics did not go together. Protest was based on morals, politics on compromise. Bob Moses answered that MFDP had to bring morality into politics, for if morality existed in politics, MFDP wouldn't have been needed in Atlantic City. Repercussions were felt far and wide. Many of the organizations that had given SNCC support began to look suspiciously at SNCC's activities. Accusations that the organization had been taken over by Communists increased.

But MFDP and SNCC did not accept defeat. SNCC, however, disagreed with MFDP's support of the Johnson and Humphrey ticket in the coming election. Nevertheless, MFDP, having pledged its loyalty to the Democratic party at the Democratic National Convention, kept that promise and worked for Johnson's election.[18] MFDP wanted to remain with the regular Democratic party and make it work for all the people. The regular Mississippi Democrats, as they had promised, carried the state for the Republican presidential candidate, Goldwater. In spite of their differences, SNCC and MFDP members still worked together to mount a new challenge against the enemies of justice.

**We go back . . . regroup and
Come to fight another day.**
—*Victoria Gray*

11. *THE FREEDOM PARTY GOES TO WASHINGTON*

The Freedom Ballot and the Atlantic City Challenge had created the kind of statewide organization that made it possible for the members of MFDP to return home and begin preparations for the November elections and a second challenge to the state. The executive committees for the five congressional districts were in place; beat, precinct, and county workers, and volunteers across the state, were well organized to go into immediate action.

MFDP, having lost in the June primary elections, made plans to enter its candidates in the November

164

regular election as independents. Section 3260 of the Mississippi Code, amended in 1942, requires persons wanting to run for congressional offices to present independent nominating petitions containing the signatures of not less than two hundred qualified registered voters in their districts.

MFDP made plans to petition for candidates from the Second, Fourth, and Fifth congressional districts: Fannie Lou Hamer from the Second, Annie Devine from the Fourth, and Victoria Gray from the Fifth.

Annie Devine, a former schoolteacher and insurance salesperson, long active in Canton, was at the time employed by CORE. Vicki Lynn, in her article "Grassroots Activists in the Mississippi Civil Rights Movement," describes Annie Devine as one who helped young people in the movement find the "blacks who were trustworthy in the Community. . . . She acted like a go-between with black male leaders [notable preachers] and young folks. Mrs. Devine was a country diplomat."[1] Her experience going door-to-door to sell insurance made her the ideal person to carry leaflets and the word to the people who were needed to register to vote.

In September, volunteers began collecting the names of qualified voters as required by Section 3260 of the state code. The regular and appropriate forms were prepared and presented, within the time limits, to Heber Ladner, secretary of state and secretary of the state board of elections. He refused to accept the forms, ruling that every signer of the petitions had to be certified as being a qualified voter by the registrar who had registered the voter.

No such verification is required in Section 3260 of the Code. Still, MFDP made the effort to obtain that certification. Some registrars refused to certify the names. Those who were certified were told they had to present receipts showing that they had paid poll taxes. These delaying tactics made it impossible for MFDP members to file their certification petitions with the Secretary of the State Board of Elections in time to meet the October 1, 1964, deadline.[2]

Why were these tactics to insure disqualification used in the regular election when MFDP had been qualified for the June primaries? Could it be that after the National Democratic Convention, the regular democrats felt that MFDP, being so well organized, and with national support, just might present a threat? Or were the election laws of Mississippi to be followed or not at random, on a whim?

Nevertheless, MFDP began to make plans to contest the election. It also planned to hold a parallel Freedom Ballot in November. Freedom Democrats spread out across the state and registered voters and set up polling places in churches, lodges, barbershops, and homes. MFDP candidates ran in all five congressional districts on the Freedom Ballot. Besides the three women already mentioned, Augusta Wheaton ran in the First district, Mildred Cosey, Evelyn Johnson, and Allen Johnson in the Third. The whites on the regular Democratic ballot were Thomas G. Abernethy, First district; James L. Whitten, Second; John Bell Williams, Third; Arthur Winstead, Fourth; and William Meyers Colmer, Fifth. Prentiss Walker ran as an independent in the Fourth district.

While the work went on, SNCC, the Council of Federated Organizations (COFO), and MFDP were going through structural and financial difficulties. Groups such as the NAACP, the Southern Christian Leadership Conference (SCLC), CORE, and the National Council of Churches pressured SNCC to be more disciplined in its organizational structure—more definite about who made policy. They wanted to know just what was the relationship between SNCC, COFO, and MFDP. There were criticisms from the press, claiming that MFDP members were not aware of the dangers of communism in the civil rights movement in the South.

These allegations angered those who for almost five years had labored in Mississippi, through deaths, threats of death, much harassment, and many hardships. They rejected the thought that they had to have Communists around to lead them by the hand. They rejected the assumption that there was no structure for making decisions and that decisions were made by people other than those directly involved in the struggle. At a meeting of the leading organizations where such allegations were made, SNCC defended its position:

> People on the scene make the decisions. It so happens that most of those on the scene are SNCC people, so SNCC plays a major role in decisions. But at Atlantic City it was the people, the MFDP, who rejected the compromise—Mrs. Hamer, Devine and Miles. Jim and Bob spoke only after Pratt, Rustin, Thomas, King, etc. It is only democratic that we have the right to present our position. The actual decision was made at a closed meeting of the delegation.[3]

Because of the Atlantic City confrontation, Joseph Rauh was no longer legal counsel for MFDP. SNCC had sought the help of the National Lawyers' Guild, an organization made up of many liberal lawyers, and its legal work was now spread among Arthur Kinoy, William Kunstler, and Morton Stavis.

Accusations became more rampant and much sharper when it was learned that SNCC had accepted the services of the National Lawyers' Guild to replace Rauh as legal counsel. The cry of Communist involvement and control was heard throughout the land. Again James Forman defended SNCC's action in relation to its struggle:

> Once we had wondered: How do you make somebody understand that when people have dedicated their lives to moving history a few steps forward, and are willing to work not for money but for a cause, and are willing to die for it, then nobody from a comfortable setting . . . can tell us: "You're soft on communism. . . . You don't have a statement in your constitution that bars people who believe in totalitarian government. . . . If you would only do that, then we could get you as much money as you need. As it is we don't know anyone who would give you money." We stopped wondering how to change those people. SNCC was breaking through the circle of fear that had been imposed on people by McCarthyism and which still lingered. . . . On freedom of association, . . . SNCC fought not only for its own freedom, but for the civil liberties of all.[4]

(McCarthyism got its name from Senator Joseph McCarthy, who from 1946 to 1957 made unfounded accusations against individuals and organizations under

168

the guise of fighting communism.)

Without support, SNCC and MFDP carried through with plans to hold their election and bring a second challenge to the state of Mississippi. From October 30 through November 2, 1964, the freedom elections were held. The results in the congressional districts were as follows:

(1) Second district: Fannie Lou Hamer—33,009
James L. Whitten (D)—59
(2) Fourth district: Annie Devine—907
Arthur Winstead (D)—4
Prentiss Walker—0
(3) Fifth district: Victoria Gray—10,138
William Meyers Colmer (D)—0.[5]

Augusta Wheaton defeated Abernethy in the First district and Allen Johnson received enough votes to challenge John Bell Williams in the Third district. Prentiss Walker received no votes.

On December 5, the five candidates who ran in the five congressional districts filed formal notices of contest, claiming the right to be seated in the United States Congress. They filed under the same rule that Congressman John R. Lynch had used back in 1880 when he appealed to Congress to decide just who had the right to become a member of that body. The rule required MFDP to file formal challenges within thirty days after the contested election. The Mississippi regular Democrats would have thirty days to answer. Following that, MFDP would have up to forty days to prove its charges with direct testimony from the people.[6]

The formal challenges declared that the Mississippi regular elections were invalid because approximately 50 percent of the population had not been permitted to vote. MFDP again documented the kinds of unconstitutional rules and regulations used by officials in Mississippi to prevent blacks from exercising their right to vote. MFDP's main concern this time was that the secretary of state had used tactics that denied three of its members a place on the regular ballot for the Mississippi congressional election of 1964.

MFDP GETS NATIONAL SUPPORT

MFDP supporters around the country began to lobby their congressmen to deny the officially named winners seats in the House of Representatives. A few days prior to the opening session of Congress, black Mississippians began to arrive in Washington. Hundreds of them were in the Capitol area, asking members of Congress to support the Challenge.

Stories spread that some government officials were frightened that the regular Democrats might not be seated. Much lobbying had been done by the administration to make sure that the House leadership would not allow the Challenge to succeed. Even though the MFDP members acted as if they knew they were going to be heard, they had many doubts.

On December 24, Congressman William Fitts Ryan, from New York City, announced that he and sixteen other members of the House of Representatives were prepared to challenge the right of the regular Mississippi Democrats to the state's Congressional seats.[7] He also agreed to open the Challenge in the House and to get support for a fairness resolution. This resolution would ask that no one be seated in the Mississippi seats until the MFDP challenge was finally decided by the House.

Congressman Ryan briefed some of the members of MFDP on the proceedings. The first thing Congress did after opening a new session was seat new members.

This time, Ryan would use the rules that had seated John R. Lynch. He would object to the swearing in of the regular Mississippi Democrats. The Speaker of the House would then ask the Mississippians to step aside while all the other new members were sworn in. Ryan himself did not know what would happen after that.

Careful plans for picketing, lobbying, and demonstrating in key places at the nation's Capitol had been coordinated by Lawrence Guyot and Michael Thelwell. Early on the morning of January 4, 1965, the day of the opening session of Congress, more than six hundred MFDP members, with several thousand other people from across the nation, gathered at the Lincoln Memorial Temple Methodist Church for a briefing on the day's events. Lawrence Guyot and Mrs. Hamer spoke. Then the group spread out to do specific tasks.

Some joined picket lines at the Justice Department. Because Congress was not in session, there was no way to lobby many of the representatives in their offices. Michael Thelwell decided to station people in the tunnel that members used to reach the House chambers.

One group of MFDP workers had been delayed by the weather and by breakdowns of their old bus, which was badly in need of repairs. They had hoped to get to Washington in time to join the demonstrations. They arrived too late. Just as Congress was about to go into session, they joined other black Mississippians in the tunnel. The new arrivals were amazed at what they saw.

Well-dressed men and a few women were approaching them and passing through. Some of the MFDP people had no idea that these men and women were members of the House of Representatives on their way to decide if MFDP representatives would be seated. Awed by the presence of the House members, they stood silently, as tall and as proudly as they could. Many were conscious of their damp, threadbare clothing and their muddy shoes, but they remembered why they were there and maintained a dignified silence. Their silent lobby proclaimed their desire to become first-class citizens.

Congressman Ryan came through the tunnel with Congressman Gus Hawkins of California. He spoke to the MFDP members and arranged passes so that they could sit in the gallery and hear the proceedings that were about to take place.

At noon the session opened. The Speaker of the House began alphabetically, following the usual procedure. He called the name of Thomas Abernethy from the First Congressional District of Mississippi. Congressman Ryan immediately jumped to his feet and objected to the swearing in of Abernethy. Ryan then stated the reason for his challenge. More than fifty members of Congress, from all sections of the House, stood, shouting out that they joined Ryan in the Challenge.

One of the lawyers for MFDP described the moment:

> We could hardly believe the sight. Nothing like this had happened on the floor of the House for many years. You could feel the wave of excitement speed through the packed galleries.
>
> Then all eyes turned toward the Speaker. What would he do? The hall was deadly quiet. Then the words came out, "According to the rules of this House, the gentleman from Mississippi will step aside until all other members are sworn in."[8]

Those who had worked so hard for this moment must have wanted to stand and cheer as each of the five men from Mississippi were told to stand aside. There must have been in the minds of most the triumphant joy that Victoria Gray expressed in a whisper to one of the lawyers: "We did it. Even if just for this moment, we did it."[9]

The triumph in the House that afternoon was, unfortunately, temporary. Carl Alberts of Oklahoma, House majority leader, put forth a resolution that would allow the Mississippi white men to be sworn in while awaiting the results of the Challenge. Congressmen Ryan and Roosevelt urged the House to reject this in favor of the fairness resolution: to seat no one from Mississippi until the Challenge had been resolved. Congressman Roosevelt argued, "They cannot win 'elections' based on murder and then claim the right to govern free men."[10]

The idea of not seating the white Mississippians was unacceptable to the leadership of both political parties. Carl Alberts immediately called for a voice vote on his resolution to seat the regular Democrats. Edith Green, congresswoman from Oregon, who had so courageously stood with MFDP at the first Challenge, now insisted upon a roll call. "Let everyone put themselves on the record on this one," she declared. A roll call in the House needed the support of 20 percent or more of the members. She received that much support, and a roll call proceeded.

One hundred forty-nine members of the House stood with Roosevelt and Ryan for the fairness resolution. Two hundred seventy-six members stood by Alberts and the regular Democrats from Mississippi.

How different from the challenge that had taken place in that same chamber eighty-five years before. On the day of the first session of the Forty-seventh Congress, the House ruled that John R. Lynch (who had been legally elected) was entitled to his seat. The vote was 125 to 71, with 95 not voting.[11] The issue then, as the issue was in the Eighty-ninth Congress of 1965, was massive disenfranchisement of black voters.

Not too far removed from the period of Reconstruction, Congress had taken seriously its responsibility to follow Article 1, Section 5 of the Constitution, which states: "The House of Representatives shall chuse [choose] their representatives and other officers."

Men like Thaddeus Stevens and Charles Sumner were present in 1880. Members elected by fraudulent and illegal practices were not permitted to govern free people then. That responsibility lessened in 1904, when Congress wanted the Supreme Court to rule on matters of elections. The Court sent the matter back to Congress. After 1904, the issue was pretty much ignored, and the disenfranchisement of blacks in the South became the rule. In the 1960s, the civil rights movement brought voting rights to the attention of the nation again.

That the Challenge to Congress had weight was a great surprise to many members of MFDP. Most claimed that it was a victory because of the results the Congressional Challenge had achieved, and they celebrated that evening. They were excited and fired up to continue the huge task that lay ahead to make the Congressional Challenge succeed.

If we understand both Challenges One and Two, we may now understand why it was necessary to give the history of Mississippi in such detail, at times revealing the most gruesome facts of the struggle. To support the Challenge, MFDP had to document all the threats of violence, intimidation, economic punishment, and terrorism directed against it. It also had to prove the systematic refusal of officials to permit African Americans the right to register and to vote. This documentation had to be presented for each congressional district, setting forth all the illegal acts committed against residents of that district. MFDP had done all this by December 4, 1964.

The five regular Democrats had thirty days to answer the charge that they were not legally elected representatives in the First, Second, Third, Fourth, and Fifth congressional districts. On January 4, 1965, after the opening session of Congress, the regular Democrats filed their answers as required by the statutes. They argued:

(1) that they [the contestees] were not properly served [delivered writs, summonses, etc.]; (2) that the contestants [MFDP] lacked standing because they were not on the [official] ballot; (3) that they knew nothing of the exclusion of blacks from the electoral process; and (4) that the Mississippi laws had not been declared unconstitutional by any court and must be presumed to be constitutional, and that any question of constitutionality was within the jurisdiction of the Supreme Court and not Congress.[12]

Congress answered the contestees with the directive that "the laws governing contested elections would apply to any questions involving the election of the members in question."[13] That clearly meant that the regular Democrats had to prepare a defense for all charges of denial, threats, and abuse, and that MFDP must have each person involved in each district sign affidavits affirming these charges. These affidavits were legal documents that had to be prepared by lawyers.

There were exactly three black lawyers in the whole state of Mississippi at that time. The cost for such legal work was astronomical. Fortunately, members of the National Lawyers' Guild responded to the request that 150 lawyers come to Mississippi and within 40 days take the depositions needed to complete the Congressional Challenge.

THE LEGAL WORK BEGINS

Given the Mississippi environment, the lawyers' work was not easy. All of the 150 could not come at the same time. Some came for one or two weeks. Some prepared witnesses with interviews for testifying or answering the questions other lawyers were likely to ask. SNCC workers and MFDP members labored to find the people and bring them to the places where depositions were taken. They were taken all over the state but in some places, there were notaries public who were unwilling to cooperate, and witnesses had to go elsewhere. Suitable places were not readily available. Churches, lodges, Tougaloo College, freedom houses that had been used as registration centers, and courthouses were made available. MFDP administered the project out of its office in Jackson.

One of the regular Democrats' lawyers was former governor James P. Coleman, representing Abernethy, Colmer, Whitten, and Williams. The officials of Mississippi were, of course, bitterly opposed to the Challenge. Some of them were called by lawyers for MFDP to testify: Heber Ladner, secretary of state; Theron Lynd, registrar; and others. Senator James Eastland complained on the Senate floor:

> It is a plot by the Communist party . . . [and] efforts of the Freedom Democratic Party, a predominately Negro group, to unseat the State's Democratic House members was a Communist planned attempt to influence the Congress of the United States.[14]

On the other hand, local officials took the Challenge seriously and cautioned citizens to curb the violence. The governor decided not to call a special legislative session, for fear the representatives would pass a series of laws that would prove the MFDP's point that the laws of Mississippi denied African Americans their rights.

The lawyers for the regular Democrats were cooperative, and the depositions were completed within the
forty-day period.

There is no need here to go into the material of
the depositions. The facts have been documented—the
murders, bombings and burnings of homes and
churches, the beatings and economic reprisals. There
were more than four hundred witnesses who testified.
Their testimony was transcribed in more than ten thousand typed pages. These pages were presented to the
U.S. House printer, who at first, under pressure from
the regular Democrats, refused to print the document.

Members of the House who had supported the
Challenge insisted on having the document printed. It
came to 3,000 pages of small print. The lawyers for
MFDP then prepared a brief summarizing the material
in 117 pages, with a 99-page appendix. This brief was
given to each member of the House Administrative
Committee and to each member of the House.[15]

Lawrence Guyot notes that there was fear that the
Challenge would succeed. President Johnson sought a
compromise: If MFDP would challenge only John Bell
Williams of the Third district, then the vote not to seat
him was available. MFDP refused.

The dates for the final hearing of the Challenge
were set for September 13 and 14, 1965. On August 6,
1965, exactly one year after the MFDP state convention
was held to choose delegates to the Democratic National
Convention, President Johnson signed the Voting
Rights Act, which became the Twenty-fourth Amendment to the Constitution. This act still did not outlaw

poll-tax payments in Mississippi, or in other southern states, for local and state elections. (The payment of all poll taxes did not end until October 1965, with the Supreme Court decision *Harper v. Virginia State Board of Elections.*)

The fanfare following this act dimmed the importance of the Challenge before Congress. There were some forty civil rights and labor groups in the Washington-based Leadership Conference on Civil Rights, headed by Roy Wilkins of the NAACP, that had, before August 6, reluctantly given support. The majority of that group were conservative and agreed with the NAACP and AFL-CIO that, with the new Voting Rights Act, the Challenge should be called off.[16]

However, many civil rights organizations still supported the work of MFDP. Such groups as the Fourth General Assembly of the Unitarian Universalists and a clergymen's lobby with every faith represented maintained their support, as, of course, did SNCC and CORE. Dr. Martin Luther King, Jr., finally convinced most groups that to dismiss the Challenge would be the same as "to dismiss the aspirations and hopes of every Negro in America and to quench the flames of his faith in our American democracy."[17]

Finally, September 13 arrived, and the Subcommittee on Elections of the House Administrative Committee met to hear arguments from both MFDP and the Mississippi regular Democrats. In violation of the rules that called for an open session, the subcommittee met behind closed doors. The regular Democrats based their case on the fact that the MFDP had not participated in the regular elections. That should have had no bearing because three of the Freedom Democrats, Hamer, Devine, and Gray, had tried to get on the ballot but had been denied. The subcommittee did not concern itself with the merits of the case; it was only interested in dismissal, which it recommended when it reported to the House on September 17, 1965.

The galleries were again filled with MFDP supporters. Many blacks from Mississippi had traveled to Washington to witness this historic occasion. They were led into the galleries by John Lewis, president of SNCC, and Dr. Robert Spike of the National Council of Churches.

The Subcommittee on Elections' report stressed that the 1965 Voting Rights Act made it unnecessary to be concerned with the main issues of the case: voting rights. Nevertheless, there was debate on the floor of the House by representatives who believed that the subcommittee had not taken the Challenge seriously. Congressman Roosevelt was in favor of a motion to submit the matter to the committee to deal with and report on the merits of the case. He stated:

> The record in the Mississippi contested election cases of 1965 brings before the House overwhelming evidence of the simple stark facts upon which these cases rest— the almost total systematic, and deliberate exclusion of the Negro citizens of Mississippi from the electoral process of the State. . . . [T]he unimpeachable facts of wholesale Negro disenfranchisement make a mockery out of the constitutional requirements that the Members of this House be chosen "by the people of the several states. . . ." The only question remaining is whether the House of Representatives of the United States will toler-

ate elections [of] Members of the House conducted under unconstitutional laws.[18]

Congressman Ryan spoke against the subcommittee's recommendation:

> After only a three-hour subcommittee hearing closed even to committee members, the committee reported on the merits of this case. The contestants were given a chance to testify, but only as to the question of standing. Despite its stated dedication to due process and its "concern that either outright dismissal of the challenge or unseating of the present Mississippi delegation would violate this precept," the committee has ruled on the substance without permitting contestants to speak on the merit.[19]

Others in the House expressed their displeasure, but the vote to recommit to the subcommittee lost, 129 to 207. The majority leader of the House asked for support of the committee and for a vote for dismissal of the Challenge. For those members who had doubts about the merits of the decision, he proposed an amendment to the resolution, eliminating a clause that stated that the Mississippians were "entitled to their seats as representatives of said districts and state." The final vote was 228 to 143, with 51 members not voting and 10 answering "present."[20]

MFDP members took their loss knowing that with the new Voting Rights Act, changes, if they came, would be slow. There was still much to do. If the changes were to be made, the Freedom Democrats would have to continue to protest to make them happen. Their first action was to file suit in federal court to delay the primary election of June 7, 1966. They felt that the 1965 Voter Registration Act had not been in effect long enough to register enough blacks to make that election legal. The court's answer: no delay. It concluded:

> The tight grip of a long dead hand is hard to break. More than one summer may pass before that grip is broken and the effect of its clasp on the present completely undone.[21]

White Mississippians were still determined to prevent blacks from participating equally in the political life of the state. Blacks registered to vote, but tactics were used to make that vote almost useless. Districts, counties, and beats were gerrymandered. That is, lines were redrawn so that whites were a majority in a district. Where there was a majority of blacks, all offices were declared "at large," allowing every person's vote in the city or state to decide the election. This insured that no black would get elected, for whites were unwilling to cast their ballots for blacks. Nevertheless, the strength that had been gained in the struggle and the faith that only the people can make a difference helped black Mississippians to continue the work. In 1968 they cooperated with a new white democratic party, Loyal Democrats of Mississippi (LDM), to oust the regular Democrats at the Democratic National Convention in Chicago. The Mississippi Freedom Democratic Party is still active in Mississippi.

CONCLUSION

The question may be asked, why is the Mississippi

Challenge (as both challenges have come to be known) considered a great event in history? The challengers did not attain their immediate goal, but they achieved a victory. To have waged the struggle made them winners. And that struggle leading up to the Mississippi Challenge, a struggle which lasted more than a century, is one that stands out in history as testimony to the desires of men and women to be free.

Through beatings, economic reprisals, bombings and burnings, even death, the indomitable will to determine their destinies kept those men and women coming back again and again to stand against tyranny. It was not just that they struggled, but that they struggled in a way that proved the power of protest based on morals. They took grave risks to prove that the ends do not justify the means. Ends and means are interwoven. If good and just results are desired, then the way one goes about achieving them must be good and just.

Many lives were lost for the right to a decent way of life in Mississippi. Wherever there is struggle for freedom, the spirited wills of such people as John R. Lynch, Fannie Lou Hamer, Medgar Evers, Bob Moses, Lawrence Guyot, Annie Devine, Victoria Gray, and the many, many more who risked loss will be represented there. Their lights shine on the dark road that leads to peace and freedom.

Hundreds of Mississippi blacks voted for the first time in
the 1966 Congressional primaries.

UPI/Bettman

SOURCE NOTES

PART ONE

Chapter 1 *Sit-Ins, Stand-Ins, Wade-Ins, and Kneel-Ins*

    1. Henry Hampton and Steve Fayer, *Voices of Freedom* (New York: Bantam Books, 1990), p. 53.

    2. Ibid., p. 57.

    3. Ibid., p. 58.

    4. Ibid., p. 54.

    5. Ibid., p. 58.

    6. Ibid., p. 59.

    7. Dianetta Bryan, "Her Story Unsilenced: Black Female Activists in the Civil Rights Movement," *Sage* 5, no. 2 (Fall 1988), p. 62.

8. Hampton and Fayer, *Voices of Freedom*, p. 60.

9. Ibid., p. 63.

10. Howard Zinn, *SNCC: The New Abolitionists* (Boston: Beacon Press, 1964), p. 34.

11. Ibid., p. 39.

Chapter 2 *Mississippi: A Land of Contrasts*

1. *Britannica Micropaedia*, 15th ed., s.v. "delta."

Chapter 3 *Cotton and Slavery*

1. John Hope Franklin, *From Slavery to Freedom* (New York: Alfred A. Knopf, 1965), p. 185.

2. Ibid., p. 186.

3. W. E. Burghardt Du Bois, *Black Reconstruction in America* (1935; reprint, Cleveland: World Publishing, 1965), p. 431.

4. Franklin, *Slavery to Freedom*, p. 187.

5. Ibid., p. 268.

6. Ibid., p. 269.

7. Bruce Catton, *This Hallowed Ground* (Garden City, N.Y.: Doubleday, 1956), p. 307.

8. Ibid., p. 307.

9. Franklin, *Slavery to Freedom*, p. 270.

10. Ibid., p. 271.

11. Ibid., p. 277.

12. Du Bois, *Black Reconstruction*, p. 89

13. John Hope Franklin, *The Emancipation Proclamation* (New York: Doubleday and Company, 1963), p. 32.

14. Ibid., p. 28.

15. Ibid., p. 279.

16. Du Bois, *Black Reconstruction*, p. 89.

17. Catton, *Hallowed Ground*, p. 308.

18. Ibid., p. 309.

19. Ibid., p. 309.

Chapter 4 *Road to Freedom*

1. B. A. Botkin, ed., Federal Writers' Project, *Lay My*

Burden Down: A Folk History of Slavery (Chicago: University of Chicago Press, 1945), p. 230.

2. Du Bois, *Black Reconstruction*, p. 638.

3. *Britannica Micropaedia*, 15th ed., s.v. "Stevens, Thaddeus." Thaddeus Stevens, a radical Republican congressman from Pennsylvania, probably did more than anyone to guarantee blacks' freedom. He served on the committee of Reconstruction and helped prepare the Fourteenth Amendment to the Constitution. He remained a staunch advocate for freedom and a friend of the freedmen even after death: He requested he be buried among African Americans in Lancaster, Pennsylvania. He wanted to "illustrate in death what he had advocated in life: equality of man before his creator."

4. Du Bois, *Black Reconstruction*, p. 276.

5. Herbert Aptheker, *The Negro People in the United States* (New York: Citadel Press, 1951), p. 635.

6. Ibid., p. 635.

7. Du Bois, *Black Reconstruction*, p. 198.

8. Ibid., p. 603.

9. Ibid., p. 604.

10. Ibid., p. 602.

11. Ibid., p. 225.

12. Ibid., p. 648.

13. Ibid., p. 652.

14. Ibid., p. 648.

15. Ibid., p. 600.

16. Ibid., p. 227.

17. Ibid., p. 229.

18. Ibid., p. 230.

Chapter 5 *Cotton and Racism*

1. Du Bois, *Black Reconstruction*, p. 432.

2. Ibid., p. 432.

3. Ibid., p. 432.

4. Ibid., p. 435.

5. Ibid., p. 433.

6. Ibid., p. 433.

7. Ibid., p. 174.

8. Ibid., p. 175.

9. Ibid., p. 333.

10. Ibid., p. 331.

11. Ibid., p. 434.

12. John R. Lynch, *Reminiscences of an Active Life—The Autobiography of John R. Lynch*. Edited by John Hope Franklin. Negro American Biographies and Autobiographies (date unknown; reprint, Chicago: University of Chicago Press, 1970), p. 50.

13. Ibid., p. 50.

14. Ibid., p. 50.

15. Du Bois, *Black Reconstruction*, p. 438.

16. Ibid., p. 436.

17. Ibid., pp. 437–38.

18. Ibid., p. 439.

19. Ibid., p. 439.

20. John R. Lynch, *Facts of Reconstruction* (date unknown; reprint, New York: Arno Press and the New York *Times*, 1968), p. 93. Reprinted from a copy in the Moorland Spingarn Collection, Howard University, Washington, D.C.

21. Lynch, *Reminiscences*, p. 92.

22. Ibid., p. 94.

23. Ibid., p. 262.

24. Ibid., p. 264.

25. Ibid., p. 266.

26. Du Bois, *Black Reconstruction*, p. 627.

27. Lynch, *Reminiscences*, pp. 92–93.

28. Morton Stavis, "A Century of Struggle for Black Enfranchisement in Mississippi: From the Civil War to the Congressional Challenge of 1965—And Beyond," *Mississippi Law Journal* 57 (1987), p. 596.

29. Du Bois, *Black Reconstruction*, p. 587.

30. Stavis, "A Century of Struggle," p. 604.

31. Lynch, *Reminiscences*, p. 341.

32. Ibid., p. 342.

33. Ibid., p. 342.

34. Ibid., p. 343.

35. Stavis, "A Century of Struggle," p. 605.

36. Du Bois, *Black Reconstruction*, p. 631.

37. Ibid., p. 634.

Chapter 6   *Many Thousand Gone*

1. Stavis, "A Century of Struggle," p. 608.

2. Neil McMillen, *Dark Journey, Black Mississippians in the Age of Jim Crow*. (Champaign: University of Illinois Press, 1989), p. 6.

3. Ibid., p. 72.

4. Ibid., p. 74.

5. Ibid., p. 83.

6. Ibid., pp. 94–95.

7. Ibid., p. 95.

8. Ibid., p. 97.

9. Ibid., p. 85.

10. W. E. Burghardt Du Bois, "The Negro Common School, Mississippi." *The Crisis* (December 1926), pp. 101–2.

11. McMillen, *Dark Journey*, p. 116.

12. Ibid., p. 113.

13. Ibid., p. 120.

14. Ibid., p. 120.

15. Ibid., p. 121.

16. Ibid., p. 114.

17. Ibid., p. 117.

18. Ibid., p. 123.

19. Ibid., p. 124.

20. Ibid., p. 125.

21. Ibid., p. 125.

22. Ibid., p. 125.

23. Ibid., p. 232.

24. Ibid., pp. 229–30.

25. Ibid., p. 234.

26. Ibid., p. 241.

27. Ibid., p. 224.

28. Ibid., p. 238.

29. John Dollard, *Caste and Class in a Southern Town* (New Haven: Yale University Press for the Institute of Human Relations, 1937), p. 317.

30. McMillen, *Dark Journey*, p. 235.

31. Dollard, *Caste and Class*, p. 331.

32. McMillen, *Dark Journey*, pp. 227–28.

33. Ibid., p. 246.

34. Ibid., p. 247.

35. Ibid., p. 245.

36. Ibid., p. 237.

37. Ibid., p. 262.

38. Ibid., p. 246.

39. Ibid., p. 251.

40. Ibid., p. 252.

PART TWO

Chapter 7   *Freedom—A Constant Sorrow*

1. McMillen, *Dark Journey*, p. 315.

2. Ibid., p. 294.

3. Ibid., p. 55.

4. James Forman, *The Making of Black Revolutionaries* (Washington, D.C.: Open Hand Publishing, Inc., 1985), pp. 279–80.

5. Lawrence Guyot and Mike Thelwell, "The Politics of Necessity and Survival in Mississippi," *Freedomways* 6, no. 120 (Summer 1966), p. 126.

6. Forman, *Black Revolutionaries*, p. 279.

7. Ibid., p. 281.

8. Stavis, "A Century of Struggle," p. 622.

9. Ibid., p. 621.

10. Forman, *Black Revolutionaries*, p. 281.

11. Hampton and Fayer, *Voices of Freedom*, p. 140.

12. Zinn, *SNCC*, p. 59.

13. Hampton and Fayer, *Voices of Freedom*, p. 141.

14. Ibid., p. 141.

15. Zinn, *SNCC*, p. 67.

16. Ibid., p. 69.

17. Paula Giddings, *When and Where I Enter* (New York: William Morrow and Company, 1984), p. 290.

Chapter 8 *Down in the Delta*

1. Giddings, *When and Where*, p. 288.

2. Forman, *Black Revolutionaries*, p. 291.

3. Zinn, *SNCC*, pp. 88–89.

4. Fred Powledge, *Free at Last?* (Boston: Little, Brown 1991), p. 475.

5. Hampton and Fayer, *Voices of Freedom*, pp. 148–49.

6. Ibid., p. 147.

7. Powledge, *Free at Last*, pp. 331–32.

8. Zinn, *SNCC*, pp. 91–92.

9. Ibid., p. 94.

10. Ibid., p. 96.

11. Guyot and Thelwell, "Politics of Necessity," p. 131.

12. Powledge, *Free at Last*, pp. 579–80.

13. Zinn, *SNCC*, p. 106.

14. Ibid., p. 111.

15. Ibid., pp. 111–12.

16. Ibid., p. 114.

17. Guyot and Thelwell, "Politics of Necessity," p. 129.

18. Doug McAdam, *Freedom Summer* (New York: Oxford University Press, 1988), p. 28.

19. Powledge, *Free at Last*, p. 562.

Chapter 9 *A Long Summer for Freedom*

1. Len Holt, *The Summer That Didn't End* (New York: William Morrow and Company, 1965), p. 154.

2. Ibid., p. 155.

3. Ibid., p. 156.

4. Ibid., p. 157.

5. Ibid., pp. 162–63.

6. Ibid., p. 45.

7. Ibid., p. 50.

8. McAdam, *Freedom Summer*, p. 68.

9. Ibid., p. 69.

10. Powledge, *Free at Last*, p. 584.

11. McAdam, *Freedom Summer*, p. 75.

12. Hampton and Fayer, *Voices of Freedom*, p. 193.

13. McAdam, *Freedom Summer*, p. 104.

14. Ibid., p. 104.

15. Holt, *Summer That Didn't End*, p. 133.

16. Ibid., pp. 105–6.

17. Ibid., p. 107.

18. Ibid., p. 110.

19. Coles, Robert, *Children of Crisis: A Study of Courage and Fear* (Boston: Atlantic, Little Brown, 1967), p. 195.

20. Ibid., p. 196.

21. Ibid., p. 202.

22. Hampton and Fayer, *Voices of Freedom*, p. 154.

23. Ibid., p. 570.

24. McAdam, *Freedom Summer*, pp. 155–56.

25. Powledge, *Free at Last*, p. 579.

26. Ibid., p. 583.

Chapter 10 *Atlantic City Bound*

1. McAdam, *Freedom Summer*, p. 82.

2. Holt, *Summer That Didn't End*, p. 165.

3. Ibid., p. 165.

4. Ibid., p. 167.

5. Ibid., p. 167.

6. Hampton and Fayer, *Voices of Freedom*, pp. 203–4.

7. Holt, *Summer That Didn't End*, pp. 170–71.

8. Forman, *Black Revolutionaries*, p. 388.

9. Ibid., p. 388.

10. Holt, *Summer That Didn't End*, p. 172.

11. Ibid., p. 174.

12. Ibid., p. 173.

13. Ibid., p. 174.

14. Ibid., p. 174.

15. Ibid., p. 175.

16. Ibid., p. 175.

17. Forman, *Black Revolutionaries*, pp. 395–96.

18. Leslie B. McLemore, "Protest and Politics: The Mississippi Freedom Democratic Party and the 1965 Congressional Challenge," *Negro Educational Review* 34, nos. 3 and 4 (July and October 1986), p. 133.

Chapter 11   *The Freedom Party Goes to Washington*

1. Vicki Lynn Crawford, "Grassroots Activists in the Mississippi Civil Rights Movement," *Sage* 5, no. 2 (Fall 1988), p. 26.

2. Stavis, "A Century of Struggle," p. 643.

3. Forman, *Black Revolutionaries*, p. 403.

4. Ibid., p. 383.

5. Stavis, "A Century of Struggle," p. 644.

6. Arthur Kinoy, *Rights on Trial* (Cambridge: Harvard University Press, 1983), pp. 269–70.

7. Ibid., p. 271.

8. Ibid., p. 274.

9. Ibid., p. 274.

10. Ibid., p. 275.

11. Stavis, "A Century of Struggle," p. 632.

12. Ibid., p. 646.

13. Ibid., p. 446.

14. Ibid., p. 650.

15. Ibid., p. 657.

16. McLemore, "Protest and Politics," p. 140.

17. Ibid., p. 140.

18. Stavis, "A Century of Struggle," pp. 662–63.
19. Ibid., p. 663.
20. Ibid., p. 664.
21. Ibid., p. 665.

BIBLIOGRAPHY

Aptheker, Herbert. *The Negro People in the United States.* New York: Citadel Press, 1951.

Asimov, Isaac. *Our Federal Union.* Boston: Houghton Mifflin, 1975.

Belfrage, Sally. *Freedom Summer.* New York: Viking Press, 1965.

Botkin, B. A., ed., Federal Writers' Project. *Lay My Burden Down: A Folk History of Slavery.* Chicago: University of Chicago Press, 1945.

Bryan, Dianetta. "Her Story Unsilenced: Black Female Activists in the Civil Rights Movement." *Sage* 5, no. 2 (Fall 1988).

Catton, Bruce. *This Hallowed Ground*. Garden City, N.Y.: Doubleday and Company, 1956.

Coles, Robert. *Children of Crisis: A Study of Courage and Fear*. Boston: Atlantic Monthly Press, Little, Brown, 1964–67.

Crawford, Vicki Lynn. "Grassroots Activists in the Mississippi Civil Rights Movement." *Sage* 5, no. 2 (Fall 1988).

Dollard, John. *Caste and Class in a Southern Town*. New Haven: Yale University Press for the Institute of Human Relations, 1937.

Du Bois, W. E. Burghardt. *Black Reconstruction in America*. 1935. Reprint. Cleveland: World Publishing Company, 1964.

———."The Negro Common School, Mississippi." *The Crisis*, December 1926.

Duster, Alfreda, ed. *Crusade for Justice: The Autobiography of Ida B. Wells*. Chicago and London: University Press, 1970–72.

Forman, James. *The Making of Black Revolutionaries*. Washington, D.C.: Open Hand Publishing, Inc., 1985.

Franklin, John Hope. *The Emancipation Proclamation*. Garden City, N.Y.: Doubleday and Company, 1963.

———. *From Slavery to Freedom*. New York: Alfred A. Knopf, 1965.

Giddings, Paula. *When and Where I Enter*. New York: William Morrow and Company, 1984.

Gillette, Williams. *The Right to Vote*. Baltimore, Md.: Johns Hopkins Press, 1965.

Guyot, Lawrence, and Mike Thelwell. "The Politics of Necessity and Survival in Mississippi." *Freedomways* 6, no. 120 (Summer 1966).

———. "Toward Independent Political Power." *Freedomways* 6, no. 246 (Fall 1966).

Hampton, Henry, and Steve Fayer. *Voices of Freedom*. New York: Bantam Books, 1990.

Holt, Len. *The Summer That Didn't End*. New York: William Morrow and Company, 1965.

Hughes, Langston, and Milton Meltzer. *A Pictorial History of the Negro in America*. New York: Crown Publishers, Inc., 1956–63.

James, Joseph A. *The Ratification of the Fourteenth Amendment*. Macon, Ga.: Mercer University Press, 1984.

Kinoy, Arthur. *Rights on Trial*. Cambridge: Harvard University Press, 1983.

Lynch, John R. *Facts of Reconstruction*. Reprint. New York: Arno Press and the New York *Times*, 1968.

———. *Reminiscences of an Active Life—The Autobiography of John R. Lynch*. Edited by John Hope Franklin. Negro American Biographies and Autobiographies. Reprint. Chicago: University of Chicago Press, 1970.

McAdam, Doug. *Freedom Summer*. New York: Oxford University Press, 1988.

McLemore, Leslie B. "Protest and Politics: The Mississippi Freedom Democratic Party and the 1965 Congressional Challenge." *Negro Educational Review* 34, nos. 3 and 4 (July and October 1986).

McMillen, Neil, *Dark Journey, Black Mississippians in the Age of Jim Crow*. Champaign: University of Illinois Press, 1989.

Meier, August, and Elliott Rendwick. *The Making of Black America*. New York: Atheneum, 1969.

Morris, Willie. *Yazoo: Integration in a Deep Southern Town*. New York: Ballantine Books, 1971.

Powledge, Fred. *Free at Last?* Boston: Little, Brown, 1991.

Rapier, Arthur, and Ira Reed. *Sharecroppers All*. Chapel Hill, N.C.: Chapel Hill Press, 1941.

Rose, Willie Lee. *Slavery and Freedom*. New York: Oxford University Press, 1982.

Rubel, David. *Fannie Lou Hamer: From Sharecropping to Politics*. Englewood Cliffs, N.J.: Silver Burdett, 1990.

Silver, James W. *Mississippi: The Closed Society*. New York: Harcourt Brace and World, Inc., 1963.

Stavis, Morton. "A Century of Struggle for Black Enfranchisement in Mississippi: From the Civil War to the Congressional Challenge of 1965—And Beyond." *Mississippi Law Journal* 57 (1987).

Warren, Robert Penn. *The Legacy of the Civil War.* New York: Random House, 1961.

Waskow, Arthur I. *From Race-Riot to Sit-In: 1919 and the 1960's.* Garden City, N.Y.: Doubleday and Company, 1966.

Williams, McCord. *Mississippi: The Long Hot Summer.* New York: W. W. Norton and Company, 1965.

Zinn, Howard. *SNCC: The New Abolitionists.* Boston: Beacon Press, 1964.

INDEX

199

Goldwater, Barry, 152,
156, 163
Goodman, Andrew,
137–138, 146–147
Gray, Victoria, 106, 107,
132, 155
and Congressional
Challenge, 165, 169,
172
Green, Congresswoman
Edith, 154, 159, 174
Guyot, Lawrence, xiv, 8,
103, 117–118, 121,
123–128
Mississippi Freedom
Democratic Party and,
131–132, 150, 171,178

Hamer, Fannie Lou, xi,
109–110, 117
Congressional Challenge
and, 165, 169, 171
Democratic Convention
and, 132, 155–156,
158, 159
Henry, Aaron, 93, 107,
113, 121–122, 124,
158–161
Humphrey, Senator
Hubert, 153–154, 156,
158, 160

jobs, 23, 30, 34, 83–84
Johnson, Governor Paul B.,
120, 126–128, 153
Johnson, President
Andrew, 31, 32, 41,
43–44

Johnson, President
Lyndon, xii, 134, 138,
178
and Democratic National
Convention, 152–156,
160–161, 162
Justice Department, U.S.,
114–115, 117, 147,
171
voter registration and,
97, 100, 106, 113

Kennedy, Senator Robert,
100, 114
King, Dr. Martin Luther,
Jr., 7, 156–157, 160,
179
King, Reverend Edwin,
121–122, 132,
158–160
Ku Klux Klan, 46, 50, 52,
59–61, 68–69, 90,
137–138

labor, need for, 66, 69–70,
81, 90
land
black ownership of, 59,
67–71
for former slaves, 23,
30, 32–34, 45, 67
Lawson, James, 2, 4, 8
legislature, Mississippi,
47–48, 50, 96, 177
Lewis, John, 3, 4–6, 8, 124
Lincoln, President
Abraham, 20–21,
24–25

201

planters, 13–17, 42–43, 44
power of, 20, 41, 45–46,
49
Plessey v. Ferguson, 58,
92–93
Police, 4–6, 79, 114, 115,
117–118, 128,
137–138
poll taxes, xii, 52, 166,
178–179
Ponder, Annelle, 105, 107,
117, 124
population, Mississippi
African Americans, 57,
69, 81, 83
slaves, 14–15

Rauh, Joseph, 130–131,
156, 157, 158, 168
Reconstruction, 43–44,
55–56, 174
religion, 3–4, 8, 34–36,
79–80, 82–83
Republicans, 44–45, 47,
48–49, 53
retaliation, by whites, 4–6,
94–95
for voter registration,
104–105, 109–111
Reuther, Walter, 130, 156,
161
Roosevelt, Congressman
James, 154, 173, 174,
180
Ryan, Congressman
William Fitts, 154,
170–172, 173, 174,
181

Schwerner, Michael,
137–138, 146–147
segregation/integration,
1–9, 54, 58, 89–90,
91–92, 95, 99
sharecropping, 3, 50–52,
59, 74, 110–111
sit-ins, 1–9, 100, 104
slavery, 14–18, 19–20, 23–26
Civil War and, 21–23,
40–41
SNCC. *See* Student
Nonviolent
Coordinating
Committee
Southern Christian
Leadership Council
(SCLC), 2, 7, 105, 107,
113, 167
states' rights, and
Mississippi, 57–59
Stevens, Thaddeus, 31, 33,
41, 43–44, 174
Student Nonviolent
Coordinating
Committee (SNCC), 9,
167–168
direct action and, 7–8,
100–103, 135
Freedom Summer and,
126–128, 138–140,
147–148
Freedom Vote and, 122,
169
Mississippi Freedom
Democratic Party and,
130, 131, 132,
162–163, 177, 179

203

SNCC (*cont.*)
voter registration and,
xii, 100–105,
106–110, 118–120,
122–124
Sumner, Charles, 31, 41,
43, 174
Supreme Court, U.S.,
57–59, 92–93, 124,
126, 174–175

tenant farmers, 65, 74–75
terrorism. *See* Violence
Thelwell, Michael, xiv,
121, 171
Thirteenth Amendment,
xiii, 40–41, 44
Till, Emmett, 10–12
Twenty-fourth
Amendment. *See*
Voting Rights Act
(1965)

understanding clause, the,
52–54, 97, 124
Union, the
preservation of, 20–21,
24–25, 26
rejoining, 43
United Auto Workers
(UAW), 130, 153, 156

Vardaman, Governor
James K., 59, 72, 77,
78, 80, 91
Violence. *See also* Ku Klux
Klan; Lynching; White
Caps

racial, 10–12, 53, 68–69,
71, 75–84, 93–94
voter registration and,
112–118, 148,
175–176, 178
voter registration, 95–99
Freedom Summer and,
135–141, 147–148
MFDP and, 165–166
obstacles to, 52–53, 96,
97
SNCC and, 100–104,
106–112, 123–126
voting rights, 41, 43–44,
46–47, 95–96
and illegal tactics,
48–49, 132–133,
165–166, 170,
174–176, 182
need for, xi, 92, 99, 135
Voting Rights Act of 1957,
95
Voting Rights Act of 1960,
96
Voting Rights Act of 1965,
xii, xiii, 178–179, 180,
181–182

Watkins, Hollis, 106, 107,
123
White Caps, 69–70
White Citizens Council, 93,
118
White Knights, 50
white volunteers, in voter
registration, 113–114,
122–124, 135–136,
138–140

ABOUT THE AUTHOR

MILDRED PITTS WALTER grew up in a small town in Louisiana, the setting for her classic story of a summer's day, *Ty's One Man Band*, and her Coretta Scott King Honor Book for young adults, *Trouble's Child*.

A trip to Africa, as a delegate to the Second World Black and African Festival of the Arts and Culture, held in Lagos, Nigeria, inspired her to write *Brother to the Wind*, a *Parent's Choice* Book for Literature.

She has also visited Cuba, as part of a delegation of writers, and China, as a guest of Friends of China, and she's walked across Russia, from Leningrad to Moscow, to take part in a peace march.

Mildred Pitts Walter's outstanding books have often been praised for their deeply felt understanding of family relationships. As a pointer *Kirkus Review* said of *Mariah Loves Rock*, "Walter tells her story lightly but with precision: her characters are fully realized, their relationships believable." The author's many honors also include the Coretta Scott King Award for *Justin and the Best Biscuits in the World* and the Coretta Scott King Honor Book Award for *Because We Are*. Her story of school integration in a southern community, *The Girl on the Outside*, was chosen as a Christian Science Monitor Best Book of the Year.